"LET ME KILL THEM!"

"No!" Ned Remington shouted, stopping them just short of killing the outlaws.

Priest started laughing. "Hey, now," he said, whooping with laughter and slapping his knees. "If this here ain't the funniest thing I've ever seen—the marshal havin' to stop his own men from committin' murder."

"No," Remington said, "that's not funny." He turned as if to walk away, then suddenly spun back, and using the butt of his pistol as a club, brought his arm across in a vicious swipe at Priest's face. The gun caught Priest in the mouth, and teeth and blood flew as the outlaw went facedown into the dirt.

"*This* is funny," the marshal said.

REMINGTON #4

LAWMAN'S JUSTICE

JAMES CALDER BOONE

AVON
PUBLISHERS OF BARD, CAMELOT, DISCUS AND FLARE BOOKS

REMINGTON #4: LAWMAN'S JUSTICE is an original publication of Avon Books. This work has never before appeared in book form.

AVON BOOKS
A division of
The Hearst Corporation
105 Madison Avenue
New York, New York 10016

Copyright © 1987 by James Calder Boone
Published by arrangement with the author
Produced in cooperation with Taneycomo Productions, Inc., Branson, Missouri
Library of Congress Catalog Card Number: 87-91497
ISBN: 0-380-75269-7

First Avon Printing: October 1987

AVON TRADEMARK REG. U.S. PAT. OFF. AND IN OTHER COUNTRIES, MARCA REGISTRADA, HECHO EN U.S.A.

Printed in the U.S.A.

K–R 10 9 8 7 6 5 4 3 2 1

Chapter One

Viewed from a distance a visitor from the East, unused to the vastness of these open prairies, might not even know it was a town. The low, brown clumps in the grassy plain might have been another group of hummocks and hills common to this country.

It was the town of Stover, Kansas, started with high hopes and ambitions by one William Stover. Stover was killed in the street of his own town by a drunken cowboy, and the town that bore his name was itself dying on the plains, probably doomed to extinction within another fifty years.

Ned Remington, big, slab-jawed, and steely-eyed, surveyed the town as he rode in off the wagon trail onto the only street. Ned was a United States marshal, Chief Marshal for Judge Samuel Parkhurst Barnstall's Federal Court in Galena, Stone County, Missouri.

Most of the time Ned's domain was the Nations, or the unorganized Indian Territory in the area some people were calling Oklahoma. It was a little unusual for him to be in Kansas, but he had a personal reason for making the trip.

Lucas Passmore was said to be in Kansas. Lucas Passmore was the man who had murdered Ned Remington's wife then raped his daughter and left her a soul-scarred shell of the vibrant young girl she once was.

Katy Remington was now a permanent resident of a convent, in the loving charge of a group of nuns who did what they could for her. The fact that she would probaly never have a normal life kept the pain fresh in Ned.

Ned had sworn vengeance against Passmore and in the three years since it happened, he never stopped hunting the elusive killer and rapist. Ned had not abandoned his other duties and responsibilities to the court . . . he was the most effective law officer Judge Barnstall had ever known. But, between cases, his time was his own, and he used that time to trace down leads grown cold, reports, unverified, and plain hunches as to where Passmore might be.

It was the pursuit of such a lead that caused him to be in Stover. He was brought here by the news that there were two men who robbed a farm house, raped and killed the farmer's wife, then raped his daughter. The description of one of the men fit Lucas Passmore.

The crime happened in Kansas and wasn't the responsibility of Judge Barnstall's court . . . but as there was a federal warrant for Passmore, Ned used that as his excuse to get involved.

The farmer, whom the men had left alive, said that the one who fit the description of Passmore was riding a black gelding with a white blaze on its face, and a white stocking on the right, rear leg. The other man was riding a roan. Ned had followed those leads to this place.

Ned had seen hundreds of towns like this. On either side of the street false-fronted shanties, a few sod buildings, even some tents, straggled along for nearly a quarter of a mile. Then, just as abrubtly as they started, they quit, and the prairie began again.

In the winter and spring the street would be a muddy mire, worked by the horses' hooves, and mixed with their droppings, so that it became a stinking, sucking, pool of ooze. In the summer it was baked as hard as rock. It was summer now, early afternoon, and the sun was yellow and hot.

Ned searched out the saloon, then saw what he was looking for tied to the hitching rail out front. Suppressing a feeling of excitement, he rode up to the saloon and dismounted. The two horses matched, exactly, the description given by the farmer. Ned went over to the two animals, patted them as he looked at them, then checked the pistol in his holster, and walked inside.

Because of the shadows, there was an illusion of coolness inside. It was an illusion only, for the dozen or so customers were sweating in their drinks, and wiping their faces with bandanas.

As always when he entered a strange saloon, Ned looked around the place. To the unsuspecting observer his glance would be one of idle curiosity. In fact it was a trained surveillance. Who was armed? What type guns were they carrying? How were they wearing them? Was there anyone here he knew? More importantly, was there anyone here who knew him, who might take this opportunity to settle some old score, real or imagined, for themselves or a friend?

Quickly, Ned saw that there were only workers and drifters here. The couple of men who were armed were young men, probably wearing their guns for show as much as anything. From the way the pistols rode on their hips, he was certain they had never used them for anything but target practice and not very successfully at that.

The saloon owner stood at the end of the bar.

There were two glasses with whiskey remaining in them, and he poured the whiskey back into a bottle, corked it, and put it on a shelf behind the bar. He wiped the glasses out with his stained apron, then set them among the unused glasses. He saw Ned step up to the bar and he moved down toward him.

"Whiskey," Ned said.

The barman reached for the bottle he had just poured the whiskey back into, but Ned pointed to an unopened bottle.

"That one," he said.

The saloonkeeper shrugged and pulled the cork from the fresh bottle.

"I'm looking for two men," Ned said.

"Mister, mostly what I do is mind my own business," the bartender said.

"They were riding the horses tied up out front. The one I'm most interested in is a big, sandy-haired man. One eyelid has been cut so it's half-closed all the time. The other, they say, has a flat nose, and a scar on his right cheek."

The barkeeper didn't say anything, but Ned noticed a slight reaction to his description.

"Last week they murdered a farmer's wife," Ned said. "and they raped his daughter."

The bartender looked up. "The murdered woman . . . would her name be Linda Sue?"

"Yes," Ned said. "Yes, that's right. Did you hear about it?"

"No, we don't get no news down this way," the saloonkeeper said. He reached under the bar and pulled out a gold locket. "A couple of hombres traded this for whiskey and two women. The one with the drooping eye said it belonged to his mother. When I asked him what his mother's name was, he said Sarah. He couldn't read, you see, and he had no idea what was inscribed here."

The bartender handed the locket to Ned. He looked on back and saw the name "Linda Sue" inscribed.

"Where are they?" Ned asked.

The saloon owner said nothing, but he raised his head and looked toward the stairs at the back of the room.

"Thanks," Ned said.

At the back of the saloon, a flight of wooden stairs led up to an enclosed loft. Ned guessed that the two doors at the head of the stairs led to the rooms used by the prostitutes who worked in the saloon.

Ned started to pull his gun, then thought better of it, and slipped out his knife instead. He had waited a long time for Lucas Passmore. He didn't want to take him with a gun. He started toward the stairs.

The dozen or more men in the saloon had been talking and laughing among themselves. When they saw Ned pull his knife, their conversation died, and they watched him walk quietly up the steps.

From the rooms above him he could hear muffled sounds that left little doubt as to what was going on behind the closed doors. Normally such sounds called forth ribald comments from the patrons below, but now there was no teasing whatever; everyone knew that a life-and-death confrontation was about to take place. No one knew why, but then, such things occurred often, and no one really cared about the reasons.

Ned tried to open the first door, but it was locked. He knocked on it.

"Go 'way, Lucas," a man's voice called from the other side of the door. "You've had your woman, now let me have mine."

Go 'way Lucas, he said. That meant Lucas was in the other room!

Ned moved to the next door, raised his foot, then kicked it hard. The door flew open with a crash and the woman inside the room screamed.

"What the hell?" the man shouted. He stood up quickly, and Ned saw with a sinking feeling that it wasn't Lucas. He heard a crash of glass from the next room and he dashed to the window and looked down. He saw Lucas just getting to his feet from the leap to the alley below.

Damn! He'd been suckered in by an old trick. Passmore deliberately used his own name when he said go away, to throw Ned off. Ned kicked out the window and started to climb onto the sill to go after Passmore.

"You sonofabitch! Who the hell are you?" the man shouted. Out of the corner of his eye, Ned saw the man come after him with a knife. He lunged toward Ned, making a long, would-be, stomach-opening swipe. Ned barely managed to avoid the point of the knife. One inch closer and he would have been disemboweled.

"I'll cut you open like a pig, you sonofabitch," the man with the flat nose said. "Who the hell you think you are bustin' in here like this?"

The man swung again and Ned jumped deftly to one side, then counter thrust. The blade of his knife buried itself in the man's neck, and Ned felt hot blood spilling across his hand. The man gurgled, and his eyes bulged open wide. Then, slowly, he slipped to the floor.

"Passmore," Ned said, kneeling beside the wounded man. "Where is he heading?"

"Who . . . who are you?" the man asked. Blood bubbled at his lips when he spoke.

"Remington. Ned Remington. I'm a United States marshal and I'm after Lucas Passmore."

"You . . . You ain't after me for killin' that farmer's wife?"

"That's something for the state of Kansas," Ned said.

"I'll be damned," the flat-nosed man gurgled. "I got myself kilt for nothin'."

"Where is Passmore?" Ned asked again.

"You . . . you the one he tole' me about," flat-nose said. "He said he made a mistake, kilt a marshal's wife an' now the marshal won't quit doggin' him."

"Where is he?"

"I reckon you'll just have to keep lookin' for him," flat-nose said.

Ned stood up angrily. He had lost valuable time trying to get the outlaw to talk. He turned and ran from the room, down the stairs, and out the front. Both outlaw horses were gone. That gave Passmore an advantage, because by switching from horse to horse, he would be able to extend his range.

Ned started after him. It was the closest he had ever been and he didn't want to let the trail grow cold.

Ned thought of his adversary as he chased him. Passmore had deliberately placed his friend in jeopardy by calling out his own name back at the saloon. Then he had taken his friend's horse so that, even if his friend had survived the confrontation, he would still have a problem. It told him a lot about the personality of the outlaw he was chasing.

Ned found the black gelding ten miles later. He found the roan five miles after that, contentedly cropping grass. He also found the body of a man stripped to his underwear. The clothes Passmore had been wearing were in a pile nearby. Passmore now had different clothes and a different horse. The trail was getting colder.

When Ned took the body into Fredonia, the sheriff asked him if he was Ned Remington.

"Yes," Ned replied.

"Judge Barnstall's sent wires out to ever' sheriff in this part of Kansas," the sheriff said. "He's got a trial comin' up in ten days. You have to be there to testify."

Ned let out a long sigh. He had no choice. His arrangement with the judge was that he could continue to search for Lucas Passmore as long as he wanted . . . but when he was needed for another case, or for a trial, he was to return as soon as he was summoned.

Ned walked over to the sheriff's wall and looked at the posters. He found one on the flat-nosed man he had killed in the knife fight.

WANTED FOR MURDER
William Elijah Anderson
alias
Flat-Nosed Willie
$1,000 reward

Ned pulled the flyer down and handed it to the sheriff.

"I guess I saved the state of Kansas a little money today," he said. "I killed this fella in a saloon back in Stover." He made the comment about saving money because, as a United States marshal, he wasn't eligible for the reward.

"Tell me, marshal, what are you doin' chasin' down these here fellas in the first place? This ain't a federal case."

"No, but I have a federal warrant on Lucas Passmore."

"I didn't know there was any federal paper on Passmore. When did that happen?"

"My warrant's three years old," Ned said.

"You've been chasing one man for three years?"

"Yes. And I'll chase him for the rest of my life, then for the next ten thousand years in hell if I have to," Ned said resolutely.

The sheriff eyed Ned curiously. "Sounds to me like that's pretty personal."

"It is," Ned said without elaboration.

The sheriff picked up the telegram he had from Judge Barnstall and looked at it for a long moment.

"Listen," he offered in an understanding voice. "I could say I haven't seen you yet. If you want, you never heard about this wire."

Ned ran his hand through his hair.

"No," he said. "I have an agreement with the judge. When he calls, I'll come. Passmore won't get away from me." He smiled a menacing smile. "Like I said, I'll get the sonofabitch if it takes me ten thousand years."

Ned Remington, freshly bathed, shaved, and shorn, presented himself to the judge in his chambers. The judge poured them each a brandy, then handed a snifter to Ned. Ned took a swallow. He could taste the controlled fire of the fruit on his tongue. After so many glasses of cheap trade whiskey, this was like nectar and he held the glass up and looked at it appreciatively.

"Like it?" the judge asked.

"Yes, I do."

The judge smiled. "This was bottled especially for Napoleon. It was sent to me by a colleague in New

York. As you might believe, I drink from this bottle very sparingly.''

"I can see why,'' Ned said. "What I don't see is why you chose to share a glass with me, now.''

The judge sat down at his desk and looked up at his chief marshal. Of course, since Ned Remington was a touch over six feet tall, the judge had to look up at him even when he was standing, though the judge was a powerfully built man in his own right.

"Maybe it was a thank you,'' the judge said.

"For what?''

"For coming when I called.''

"That's our agreement.''

"I know it is. But I also know how badly you want that man.''

"I want him, yes,'' Ned said. "But every time we bring in a killer, or a rapist, I feel like I'm getting a little piece of him. My day will come, Judge. In the meantime, I get a great deal of satisfaction from my work.''

"I'm glad you see it that way, Ned.'' The judge took out two cigars from his carved box. He handed one of them to Ned. The two men bit off the ends, then lit their smokes.

"I don't see the trial taking more than two or three days at the most,'' he said. "I'll need you to testify, then to see to order during the hanging.''

"All right.''

"Then you'll be going out after Passmore again?''

"No,'' Ned said. "I reckon not. For the time being, the trail's grown cold. I'll get wind of him again, and when I do, if I'm free, I'll go after him.''

"Ned, I don't have to tell you that nothing would give me more pleasure than to have that sonofabitch come before my bench,'' the judge said. "I know it won't bring your wife back, or ease the suffering of your daughter, but, oh, how I would like to hang him. By the way, how is Katy? Have you seen her since you got back?''

"I saw her this morning," Ned said. "She's speaking now. You don't know what a joy that is after so many months of terrible silence. The Mother Superior thinks that, with loving care, she could come almost all the way back.''

"We can all pray for that day,'' the judge said.

"That I do, Judge. That I do,'' Ned said.

Chapter Two

Fifteen-year-old Lincoln Nelson held his head under the mouth of the pump while he worked the handle. Ice-cold, deep-well water cascaded over him, washing away the dirt and sweat from an afternoon of hard work in the field. He reached for the towel he had draped across the split-rail fence, but it was gone. He heard a girl's giggle.

"Linda," he said angrily. "Gimme the towel you took."

"What towel?" Linda teased.

Lincoln rubbed the water out of his eyes then opened them and saw his twin sister standing there, holding the towel behind her back. She was smiling at him.

"If you don't want me to dry my face on your dress, you'll gimme that towel," Lincoln growled.

"Oh, you mean this towel?" Linda said. She handed the towel to him.

"Very funny." Lincoln took the towel and began drying his face. Linda stood beside him, examining her fingernails. Lincoln knew his sister well enough to know that she was about to ask him for something.

"All right, what is it?" Lincoln asked.

"What do you mean?"

"You want something. What is it? My pocket knife?"

"What would a woman want with a pocket knife?" Linda asked.

Lincoln chuckled. "Woman? You wanted to use it yesterday. Did you become a woman in one day?"

"Lincoln, Papa won't let me go to the church picnic with Tommy Rawlings," Linda pouted. "He says I'm too young."

"You are too young," Lincoln said.

"Too young? I'm the same age as you, Lincoln Nelson."

"That don't make no difference, you're a girl."

"I'm not a girl, I'm a woman, near 'bout," she said. She leaned against the split-rail fence and thrust her hip out, proudly displaying the developing curves of her young body. "You tell papa to let me go to the picnic with Tommy. Papa'll listen to you."

"Ha! In a pig's eye he will," Lincoln said. He lay the towel back across the rail. "What's for supper? I'm 'bout starved."

"Breaded pork chops and fried potatoes," Linda said. "And I made 'em myself."

"They'll probably poison me," Lincoln teased.

Brother and sister walked back up the path to the house, following the rich aroma of fried pork. Lincoln pushed the door open, then came to a complete halt, his eyes wide with confusion.

There were three strange men in the kitchen. One was stocky and red-haired, with stitchmarks over his right eyebrow. He was standing behind Perry, Lincoln's father, holding a gun to his father's head. Another was medium sized, dark complexioned, with a long, hooked moustache. He had a mashed nose and long black hair which hung in braids down his back. The dark one was holding a knife to their mother's throat. The third, a tall, thin man with a ripped earlobe on his left side, was standing behind the table eating a pork chop which he held in his left hand. Bits of grease and breading clung to his chin.

"Well, now, would you lookee at this little thing? She'll do fine. She'll do real fine." He looked at Linda with eyes that shined in unabashed lust.

"Who are you?" Lincoln asked. "What are you doing with my ma and pa?"

"Boy, you ain't needed," the tall one said. He pulled out his gun and before anyone could say a word, pulled the trigger. The gun roared as a wicked flash of flame jumped from the barrel of the gun and a cloud of smoke billowed out over the table. The bullet hit Lincoln in the forehead, then burst out from the back of his head, carrying with it bits of bone, skin, and brain matter. Heavy drops of blood splattered from Lincoln's wound onto Linda's face and fanned out onto the bodice of her dress.

"Lincoln!" she screamed, as her brother, already dead, fell to the floor. She dropped to her knees beside him and put her hands on his face, trying desperately to deny what she was seeing with her eyes.

"Murderers!" Lincoln's mother yelled. She tried to stand up, but the dark one shoved her back down in her chair, then cut a nick in her face with the tip of his knife. A bright red stream of blood began flowing from the cut.

"Leave her alone!" the father shouted, but his shout was cut off by a blow to the back of his head as the red-haired man brought his gun down sharply.

Perry Nelson opened his eyes and saw the stars of a midnight sky. For a moment he wondered where he was, and why was he sleeping outside. Then he felt the pain in his head, and recalled vividly seeing his son murdered. He tried to get up, but discovered that he was tied.

"Are you all right?" Elaine asked.

"What's going on?" Perry asked. "Where are we?"

"We're in the back of a wagon," Elaine said. "They're taking us somewhere."

"Lincoln?"

"He's . . . he's dead," Elaine said.

"Linda?"

"I'm here, Papa," Linda said. Perry struggled to turn over and saw his daughter sitting against the side of the wagon, her knees drawn up, her arms wrapped around her legs.

"Are you hurt?"

"No."

"You're not tied," Perry said. He looked toward the wagon seat and saw the breed driving. The other two were riding just ahead of the wagon, leading the breed's horse.

"Linda, slip down over the back," Perry said. "Slip down and run away."

"No," Linda said. "Papa, they said if I tried to run away they'd kill you and Mama."

"They'll probably do that anyway," Perry said. "Go on, get away."

"I can't," Linda said. "Papa if I run and they kill you, I . . . I wouldn't want to live."

Perry struggled until he was finally able to sit up. He looked around outside the wagon, caught the gleam of moonlight on a stream of water. "That's the Grand River," he said. He looked around some more, getting her bearings. "Yes. And that's the Boston Mountains. We're in the Cherokee Nation. Why did they bring us down here?"

"I don't know," Elaine said. "Oh, Perry, what are they going to do?"

"Hey!" the breed called, and the two men stopped, then came back to the wagon.

"What do you want?"

"The man is awake."

The tall one came back to look down into the wagon. He rubbed his ripped ear as he studied his three prisoners. "Yeah, well, we're out of Missouri. This is as good a place as any," he said.

"Yeah," the red-haired one replied. "I been waitin' for this. Lordy, I been waitin' for this."

"Get out of the wagon, girl," the tall one said.

"Papa?" Linda said in a quiet, frightened voice.

"Don't be goin' to your papa, girl, they ain't a damned thing he's gonna be able to do about it but watch."

"No!" Perry said, realizing then what the men had in mind. "No, leave her alone!"

The breed hit Perry in the face with his fist. Perry had no way to ward off the blow, no way to dodge it. His eye puffed shut, and his head banged back against the side of the wagon.

"The girl's mine," the tall, thin one said.

"Well, hell, you gonna share with us, ain't you?" one of the others asked.

"Yeah," the tall one said. "Yeah, I'm gonna share with the rest of you," he said. "Soon's I'm finished with her you can have all you want."

"Please," the mother begged. "Leave her alone. If . . . if you must do something . . . take me."

The stocky red-haired man laughed. "Oh, you'd like that, wouldn't you, woman." He rubbed himself. "I spec you'd like that a lot, gettin' yourself some real men 'stead o' the farmer you're married to. But we ain't interested in you. We want somethin' young . . . something purty."

"No . . . please, no," the mother begged.

"Woman, you jus' gonna have to take your pleasure from watchin'," the tall one said in a low, gravelly voice. Then, smiling evilly at the girl, he grabbed himself. "Look what I got for you."

Perry yelled his defiance at them, and the leader, afraid that someone might be passing by, nodded at the breed to hit him again. This time Perry went out from the blow. When he regained consciousness a while later, he saw his daughter lying on the ground, naked, her legs spread wide. He looked over at his wife, Elaine. She, too, was naked and her body was covered with cuts and welts, evidence of the torture she had undergone while Perry was unconscious.

The tall thin one, apparently just finished, was buckling his pants as he stood over Linda's prostrate form. He rubbed the back of his hand across his mouth.

"Well, now, I got 'er all broke in for you. Who's gonna be next?"

"My God! You . . . you *raped* her!" Perry said, realizing what had happened while he was out.

"Naw, it warn't rape. Jus' a little friendly lovin', that's all."

The Mexican half-breed grunted something, then dropped his trousers to his ankles and came down over the young girl.

"No! No!" Perry shouted.

"Put a gag on him," the leader said. "The woman too. We can't keep knockin' him out to keep 'im quiet. 'Sides, I want him to watch."

Linda lay unmoving beneath the breed. Her eyes were open but they had a glazed-over, blank look, as if her soul had died. She didn't make one sound as the breed grunted out his evil pleasure on her.

*   *   *

Keeler Ross, a neighbor to the Nelsons, swung
down from his horse and tied it at the hitching rail.
He could hear the cow bawling in the barn, and he
wondered why it hadn't been milked yet. The sun
had been up for two hours now, the cow should've
been milked a long time ago.

Keeler walked up to the front door and knocked.

"Hello, Perry," he called. "Perry, Mrs. Nelson,
it's Keeler Ross. Is anyone home?" He knocked
again.

Keeler waited for a moment, then started back to
his horse. The cow bawled again, and he stopped and
looked toward the barn. It wasn't like the Nelsons to
leave a cow unmilked like that. He walked around
the side of the house, by the marigolds and petunias
Mrs. Nelson had so carefully cultivated.

"Mrs. Nelson?" he called again. "It's me, Keeler
Ross."

When Keeler reached the back corner of the house
he heard the sound of a hundred or more buzzing
flies. He stopped cold. He had heard buzzing flies
before, but he had not heard them with this intensity
since Shiloh. On the day after the first big battle,
hundreds of bodies were left lying on the battlefield.
When Keeler looked at the bodies from a distance,
they were black and moving from the thousands of
flies that were drawn to the feast. The flies made the
same sound then as he was hearing now.

Keeler stopped in his tracks. He wasn't carrying a
gun but if he had been, he would have drawn it now.
Instead, he took a deep breath, then began to creep
very slowly around the corner of the house. He looked
toward the back door, then gasped. Lying half out of
the back door, with his head on the bottom step, was
young Lincoln Nelson. Lincoln's eyes were open and
unseeing, there was a hole in his forehead, a bigger

hole in the back of his head. It was Lincoln who had drawn all the flies.

Keeler slipped silently along the back of the house, then peeked inside. He saw the table set for a meal. There were pork chop bones on the tablecloth, on the floor. The meal had been eaten, but not from the plates, which were still clean in their place. Cautiously, he stepped through the door, then began looking through the house. There was not one trace of the rest of the Nelson family.

When Jay Rogers saw the wagon sitting there, he wondered who it belonged to. He was sure it didn't belong to any of the people in or around his village. It looked like a white man's wagon, but if so, what was it doing here? He clucked at his horse and rode toward it, keeping his eyes open and his ears alert. When he got closer he saw that there were two people in the back. At first he thought they were sleeping, but as he got closer, he saw that they were tightly bound. He also realized that the woman was totally naked.

He urged the horse into a gallop for the last several yards, then he jumped down to check them. They were both alive. He unrolled his bedroll and spread the blanket on the woman's naked body. When he did, he heard a groan coming from the man's lips. Quickly, he untied the man, then the woman. He brought his canteen over, sprinkled some water on their faces, then when they came to, offered them a drink.

"Linda," the man said, gasping and choking as he came to. "Where's Linda?"

"Your wife is here," Jay said.

"No, my daughter," the man said.

Jay looked around, then he saw her, lying over in

some tall grass. She, too, was naked, and Jay feared she might be dead. He hurried over to her and saw that she was not only alive, she was conscious. She was staring straight up, humming a little tune. The dark bruises on her legs and thighs provided graphic evidence as to what had happened to her.

Jay walked back to his horse and got his poncho, then draped it across the girl.

"Are you all right, girl?" he asked.

Linda interrupted her humming and looked at the man who was tending to her. Though he was obviously an Indian, her eyes seemed to take no note of the fact. After a long moment of looking at him, she looked away and began humming the little tune again.

Jay walked back to the wagon where Perry was giving his wife a drink of water. One of Perry's eyes was completely closed, his lip was puffed out, there was blood on his face, in his hair.

"Who did this terrible thing?" Keeler asked.

"I never saw them before," Perry mumbled. "There were three of them."

"White men?"

"Two were. I don't know about the third. Maybe Indian, maybe Mexican."

"Why were you here, in The Nations?"

"We weren't," Perry said. "We were in our own house in Missouri. They came in while Lincoln and Linda were outside. I heard the door, thought it was the kids. When I looked up they were standing there, holding guns on us. They held Elaine and me in the chairs until the kids came in from washing up for supper. They . . . they shot Lincoln right off, then they knocked me out. When I came to I was tied up in the back of the wagon. They brought us here, then they took Linda out and they . . . they . . ."

"You don't have to say," Jay said.

"They made us watch," Perry sobbed. "The dirty bastards made us *watch*."

"It's a bad thing to have happen here, in The Nations," Jay said.

"What I can't stand is the thought that the bastards will get away with it."

"No," Keeler said. "They will be caught, and punished."

"How? If they leave The Nations, the Indian police won't be able to go after them. And I can't go to the sheriff back home. He'll just tell me it's out of his jurisdiction."

"We can send word to Marshal Ned Remington," Jay said.

"Remington? The U.S. marshal who rides for Judge Barnstall's court?"

"Yes. My cousin, Tom Beck, rides for the marshal. If you wish, I will send word to him."

"Yes," Perry said. "Yes, do that. I want them to pay for what they did. I want them to hang."

Chapter Three

The trial Ned had come back from Kansas for was over. Justice was served by sending an outlaw to his Maker, and a lazy, summer tranquility had settled over the town of Galena, Missouri. With the trail of Lucas Passmore grown cold, Ned decided to spend some time in town, visiting his daughter on a daily basis, and tending to some of the paperwork that had piled up in the U.S. marshal's office.

This morning his chair was on the stoop, tipped back against the front wall of Bessie's Restaurant. He had come outside after his breakfast of flapjacks and sausage to smoke a cigarette and drink a cup of coffee. The casual passer-by would take no more notice of him than he would of Will Hampton's old collie-dog sleeping in the morning sun in front of the hardware store next door.

Perhaps the visitors to Galena didn't notice Ned, but Ned noticed every one of them. In spite of the appearance of ease, he had missed nothing of note on the main street in this small, Missouri town. He saw two men walking toward the livery, and by their dress and manner, knew they were teamsters for a freighting outfit out of Springfield. Across the street a man stepped out of the Galena Hotel and set his carpet bag on the front porch. The man was wearing a brown suit and vest, and he pulled a gold watch

from his vest pocket and looked at it importantly.
Ned hadn't met him, but knew he was a drummer,
probably from Joplin, since he was obviously waiting
for a stage and the next one due was headed for
Joplin.

This early summer morning, with the sun warm
and the sky clear, Ned was very much at peace with
himself. Despite this contentment, however, there
was always a part of him that remained alert to any
possibility. He never took anything for granted, and
would not allow himself to be lulled into a false
sense of security.

Experience as a United States marshal had taught
Ned to take his ease whenever he could, but to
always be prepared for a violent shattering of his
peace. As a result, even when he was at rest, his face
told the story of years of harsh experiences. He was a
big man, with a strong chin and steel blue eyes that
had an icy glint, even in the palest light. Those
eyes had been the last thing many a hardened gun-
fighter had seen when they made the mistake of
challenging Ned Remington.

Ned had seen the Indian arrive about fifteen minutes earlier. From the Indian's dress and the way he
rode, he knew he was from The Nations, and he
figured the Indian was coming to see Judge Barnstall.
He didn't allow himself to become overly curious
about it, he figured that if there was any message for
him, the Judge would send for him soon enough.

Soon enough arrived. Ned saw one of the court
clerks come down the stairs from Barnstall's second-
story office, then shield his eyes against the morning
sun to look up and down the main street. Ned figured
the clerk was looking for him, so he tipped his chair
forward, stood up, and started toward the courthouse.
He was half-way to the courthouse before the clerk

saw him, then came to deliver the message. Ned was right. Barnstall wanted to see him.

There were three men besides the Judge in Barnstall's office. The Indian Ned had seen, Tom Beck, one of Ned's deputies, and who was himself part Cherokee, and Russell Milsap, an assistant prosecutor down from St. Louis to watch and learn in Judge Barnstall's court. Milsap seemed like a decent enough sort, though he was young, curious, and green as grass.

"This is Jay Rogers," Barnstall said, introducing the Indian. "He's Tom Beck's cousin."

"Rogers," Ned said, nodding toward him.

"Mr. Rogers has brought us a story of a terrible event thay took place down in the Cherokee Nation, on the Grand River. You want to tell the marshal what you told me, Mr. Rogers?"

Jay Rogers told of riding upon the Nelson family wagon to find the young girl raped, the parents tortured. The son had been murdered back at the farm before the family was taken, and the family was back home now, burying their dead and nursing the daughter who was pathetically addled by the horrible experience. Rogers finished by saying that the criminals were white men, and had done this against a white family that they took across the border, but their action was so brutal that even the Cherokees were shocked by it, and wanted the men brought to justice.

"He thought of his cousin here, so he brought the case to us," Judge Barnstall said, taking over from there. Barnstall pulled a cigar from his humidor and lit it before going on. He took several puffs, then with the smoke billowing around his head, continued.

"Ned, I'm issuing you three John Doe warrants. These men have bragged that they'll never be taken

alive." He pulled the cigar out and examined the end
for a moment, then looked at Ned through narrowed
eyes. If there's any trouble, you kill them. I want
them to hang, but if you can't bring them in, then
I'm giving you wide leeway in this case."

"All right, Judge," Ned said. He looked at Tom
Beck. "Any reason you can't come with me, Tom?"

"I was hoping you'd ask," Tom answered. Beck
had steely blue eyes, hair straight as straw with a
tinge of red, and a sharp, hooked nose. He was short
and spare, but people who thought that gave them
an advantage in a fight were sorely mistaken.

"I'd like to take Frank Shaw, too," Ned said.

Frank Shaw had half a dozen scars from as many
bullets, but Ned knew him to be a man who never
backed down . . . a good man on the trail and a good
man with a gun.

"All right by me. I want you to take Milsap with
you too," the judge said, pointing to the young
assistant prosecutor.

"Are you serious?"

"Yes," Barnstall said. He stuck the cigar back
into his mouth and looked over it at Milsap. "The
boy's come here to learn, I can think of no better
lesson than to have him go with you on this job.

"I won't get in the way," Milsap said quickly.

"You won't get in the way? Boy, there's more to
it than just staying out of the way," Ned said. He
sighed. "Can you shoot a pistol?"

"I'm not a proficient marksman if that's what you
mean. But I do know the mechanics involved," Milsap
answered. "I know that pulling the trigger snaps a
firing pin against a primer, thus igniting the propellant charge."

". . . *thus igniting the propellant charge?* Jesus
Christ, Judge, what the hell is this?"

"He's going, Ned," Barnstall said in a quiet, resolute voice.

Ned sighed, and looked at the young lawyer.

"All right," he said. He pointed at him. "But you just make damn sure when you 'ignite the propellant charge' that you know which way you're pointing the pistol."

"I'll be very careful," Milsap promised.

Ned looked over at Jay Rogers. "Do you have descriptions?"

"Yes," Rogers said. He described each of them as they were described to him by the father of the girl who was raped.

"I've heard tell of these men," Tom Beck added.

"Do you know any names?"

"No. But they work mostly between Joplin and Independence, rob only at night, do a little rustlin' sometimes. And the Nelsons ain't the first ones they've took down to the Nations with them. They done this before, and ever'time they do it, they make the people hurt real bad. They the kind that likes to see other folks hurt."

"They sound like real nice people," Ned said sarcastically. "I'm going to enjoy bringing them in."

"I looked around out by the wagon. They didn't leave much trail, they're going to be hard to track," Jay Rogers suggested.

"But not too hard for you, huh, Tom?" Ned asked. Tom was a known tracker who didn't give up. It was said that he could track a mouse across rock.

"I reckon I'll find 'em," Tom said.

"I don't care how hard they are, I want these men caught," Barnstall said

"Don't worry, Judge. We'll get them," Ned promised. He rubbed his chin and looked at Tom Beck. "Tom, if they spend much time in the Nations, they surely must have a few camps hid out down there they can go to.''

"I was just a'thinkin' that self-same thing," Tom said.

"I want you to scout along the Oklahoma-Kansas border, see what you can find. Meet me in Baxter Springs two weeks from today."

The deputy got up and left without another word. He knew what had to be done . . . there was no sense in hanging around talking about it.

Ned looked over at Milsap. "You," he said. "Get out of that court-room suit and into some duds you can trail with. I'm going after Frank Shaw. When you're ready, meet me at the livery stable."

"Where are we going, Marshal?" Milsap asked eagerly.

"You just put your horse's head on my horse's rear and stay there," Ned said. He heard Barnstall chuckle as he went downstairs to find Frank Shaw.

The stage for Joplin was pulled up in front of the Galena Hotel. The drummer was the only passenger so he stood on the porch while the baggage was being loaded. If there had been more passengers, the drummer, as an experienced stage-traveler, would have boarded first to make certain of the most comfortable seat. As it was, he would stay outside for as long as necessary, since the trip would keep him in the coach long enough.

A bow-legged, gray-haired, bewhiskered man was loading several black cases onto the stage. He looked old, bent, and tired, hardly up to the task, yet he seemed to handle the cases with ease as he picked them up and tossed them to the driver on top.

"I say, my good man, be careful with those cases,

won't you? All my samples are in them. You aren't handling bags of seed, you know.''

The bow-legged man with gray hair and whiskers looked over at the drummer, then squirted a stream of tobacco at the drummer's feet. He tossed another case up to the driver who stowed it on top of the coach.

''I said *be careful*. And watch where you expectorate,'' the drummer said. ''Had you gotten tobacco on my trousers, you would have been in for a good thrashing.''

The baggage loader didn't say a thing, didn't even look at the drummer as he limped over toward another piece that was being shipped. His shirtsleeves were rolled up and there were puffy patches of scar-tissue on both arms. They were just about the size of bullet holes, and in fact, that was what caused the wounds.

The baggage handler looked up as Ned approached. There was a question in his eyes.

''Got a job,'' was all Ned said.

''Let me get my horse and gear,'' the baggage handler said. He set the case down and started down the street toward the livery. Ned knew that he kept a room there.

''Wait a minute, my good man, wait a minute here!'' the drummer called to him. ''You can't just walk off like that. My cases aren't loaded.''

''If you want 'em to go on this stage, mister, you'll throw 'em up here yourself,'' the driver called down to him.

''I will *not*.'' the drummer said indignantly.

''Makes no never-mind to me,'' the driver said. ''I can toss these back down just as easy.''

''No, no. I'll hand them up to you,'' the drummer said. He looked toward the baggage handler who was limping down the street. "Well, I like that. Just who the hell does he think he is, walking off like that?"

"He thinks he's Frank Shaw," Ned said.

"What? What would make him think a fool thing like that?"

"I reckon 'cause he *is* Frank Shaw," Ned said.

The drummer grew white in the face. He put his finger on his collar and pulled it away as he looked down the street toward the rather ordinary-looking man who was limping toward the livery.

"Look here, are you telling me he is *the* Frank Shaw?" the drummer asked.

Like all of Ned's deputies, Frank Shaw had brought his own reputation to the job. None of them were more feared than Frank Shaw.

"That's what I'm telling you."

"I don't get it. What's he doing here?"

"He's one of my deputies."

"No," the drummer said. "I mean, what's he doing working at a stage depot, carrying bags?"

"It's honest work," Ned said.

"Yes, but why would a man like Frank Shaw do such a thing?"

"A man's got to make a living some way," Ned said. "The court only pays my deputies when they're actually on a case."

"I'll be damned. Here I was, spoutin' off to him like that. He could'a shot me."

"I doubt it," Ned said. "He has to buy his own bullets, he wouldn't want to be wasting one on a fool like you."

Leaving the drummer standing there with his mouth open, Ned started down to the livery to get his own horse ready, and to wait for young Milsap. He put some jerky, beans, coffee, and two extra boxes of ammunition in the saddle bags. He filled his canteen at the pump, and was just saddling his horse when Frank came from the back, leading his horse. Frank was all ready to go.

"What have we got?" Frank asked.

Ned filled him in on what happened, including the judge's permission to bring them in dead if that was the only way they could bring them in.

"All right," Frank said. "You got a particular place in mind you want me to try?"

"I want you to go over to Joplin," Ned said. "If you can't find the men, then find out what you can about them. We'll meet up in Baxter Springs two weeks from today."

Frank nodded, then mounted his horse, just as Milsap arrived, carrying three big carpet bags with him.

"I'm all ready, Marshal," Milsap said.

Ned looked at all the stuff he was carrying with him, then sighed. "You got a bedroll in there?"

"Sure."

"Some jerky? Beans? Coffee?"

"I've got all that, plus bacon, flour, several cans of peaches, sugar and powdered milk. I've also got . . ."

Before Milsap could finish telling what all he had, Ned turned the young prosecutor's bags upside down, dumping the contents. He pulled out the jerky, beans and coffee, then pointed to it and the bedroll. "Get that on your horse," he said. "Leave everything else."

"I thought . . . I thought you said we'd be on the trail a while."

Ned swung up onto his horse and started out. "I'm heading east," he said. "When you get your horse saddled, catch up with me."

"But I . . . wait!" Milsap called.

"And don't take all day," Ned called back.

Milsap took one more look toward Ned, then, realizing that Ned was actually riding off and leaving him, started hurrying through the pile of junk that Ned had dumped. This was not going to be pleasant, he thought. This was not going to be pleasant at all.

Chapter Four

Clouds had been building up all day and when the sun set and the ground started giving off its heat, the rain started. Frank Shaw was still a good hour away from Joplin so there was nothing he could do but get under his slicker, then hunker down in the saddle for the rest of the trip.

There was a banner spread across the street as Frank entered Joplin.

"Founders' Day Fair, July 20, 21, 22. Races, wrestling, patriotic speeches."

One corner of the banner had come loose and the banner was furled like a flume so that a solid gush of water poured from the end.

The first thing Frank did after he reached town was go to the livery to get his horse out of the weather. His horse picked his way across the muddy, horseapple-strewn street toward the bright, cheery lights of Kimo's Saloon.

A long board of wooden pegs was nailed along one wall of the saloon, about six feet from the floor. Frank, after dumping the water from the crown of his hat, hung his slicker on one of the pegs to let it drip dry. He looked around the saloon. A card game was in progress near the back, some earnest conversation was going on up front. There were three men at the bar, and one bar-girl, over-weight, with bad teeth

and wild, unkempt hair, stood at the far end. She
smiled at Frank, but getting no encouragement, stayed
put.

"What'll it be, mister?" the bartender asked, making a swipe across the bar with a sour-smelling cloth.

"Whiskey, then a beer," Frank said. He figured to
drink the whiskey to warm himself from the chill of
the rain, then drink the beer for his thirst. His hip
was hurting and he rubbed it. That wound had come
from a run-in with one of Bloody Bill Anderson's
ex-riders. Frank took a bullet in the hip, then shot the
man right between the eyes. The doctor claimed he
had taken all of the bullet out, but Frank didn't
believe him. Sometimes, like now, Frank could feel
that it was still there.

The whiskey was set before him and he raised it to
his lips, then tossed it down. he could feel its raw
burn, all the way to his stomach. When the beer was
served he picked it up, then turned his back to the bar
and surveyed the room. He listened in on the conversation.

". . . .what they tell me, anyway," one of the
men said. "They was three of 'em . . . one of 'em
was a breed, come out to John Miller's place. They
took three or four smoked hams, some beans, flour,
side of bacon. They damn near cleaned him out
without so much as a by your leave."

"They didn't pay him anything?"

"Not one red cent."

"Could be them was the same three that took a
couple of horses from over to Sam Hawkins' farm,"
another said. "Didn't hear nothin' 'bout no breed,
but one of 'em had a ear they say is ripped up pretty
bad, like as if he run into a bear, or got it cut up in a
fight or somethin'."

Frank walked over to the table, and pointed to an

empty chair. "Just rode in from Galena," he said. "Thought maybe I'd join in with the jawin' if you're of a mind."

"Sure thing, mister, sit yourself down," one of the men invited. A good jaw session was more entertaining than a card game, and when a stranger from another town offered to join in, it opened up new stories and news from other places. Frank knew that, and often used it as a means of gathering information. As a nosy "jawboner" he would be told things that a deputy marshal would never hear.

"Over Galena way, huh? Would you be knowin' Fred Loomis?"

"Sure do," Frank said. "Pretty good barber, not very good at horseshoes."

"Haw!" the questioner said. "Fred's just the champeen, that's all," he told the others so they would appreciate Frank's joke.

Frank knew that this was a test, to see if he really was from Galena.

"What do you do over that way?"

"Work for the stageline," Frank said. "Hostler, baggage handler. The name's Frank."

"Good honest work," one of the men at the table said. "I'm Paul, this here is Abner, that's Tom."

Frank leaned back in his chair and nodded a greeting, while the men looked him over. There was nothing out of the ordinary about him. He was wearing a gun, but it was a rather plain-looking Colt .44 with a maple handle. The handle was cracked, but the metal part of the gun looked well maintained.

None of the other men at the table were wearing guns, but it wasn't that unusual for Frank to be wearing one. He said he worked for the stageline, he probably had to watch over the strong box occasionally. Also he'd just ridden over here and it was not unwise to carry a gun when on the trail.

"I overheard you talking about some men stealing horses and the like," Frank said. "Maybe you'd like to hear a bit of news that I picked up."

"About these three men?"

"Could be. You said one of them was a breed?"

"Yeah, wears his hair in long braids. He's got hisself a Mexican-style mustache though . . . somethin' you don't see Indians with. So I figure he's prob'ly half Indian an' half Mexican," Abner said.

"And another has a ripped ear?" Frank asked.

"Yeah, that's what I hear," Tom said.

"All right, that ties up with what I heard. Now, the third one of those galoots is a stocky, red-haired fella with stitchmarks over his right eyebrow."

"They been over Galena way?"

"Not exactly," Frank said. "But the story come to us over there." Frank went on to tell how the three men killed the Nelson boy, kidnapped the rest of the family, took them into the Nations, and raped the daughter. He pulled no punches, painting the deed as black as he could to get these men angry over the crime.

"That there's the most awful thing I ever heard of," Paul said "And what with Quantrill, Anderson, and the bunch during the war, I seen some awful things."

"Well, what's the law gonna do about it?" Abner asked. "They gonna catch 'em?"

"I reckon they're gonna try," Frank said.

"Try, hell. Catchin' 'em is their job."

"They don't even have names for 'em," Frank said.

Abner scratched his chin and squinted his eyes.

"Say, you know who might know somethin' 'bout this?" he asked.

"Who?"

"Wyland. Lou Wyland."

"Wyland? Aw, go on. He's drunk near 'bout all the time," Paul said.

"I know, but he's rode with some pretty rough people, and I hear tell that he was runnin' with a bunch that used to hide out down in the Nations," Abner insisted.

"Where is this Wyland?" Frank asked, trying not to show more than undue curiosity.

"First thing to do is look under the tables, make sure he ain't passed out under one of 'em," Tom said, then they all laughed.

"I was just thinkin'," Frank went on. "If we could find out these folks' names, we could tell the law. That might help a bit."

"Yeah," Abner said. "Yeah, you got a point there, Frank. Hey, Billy," he called to the bartender, "you seen Wyland around?"

"Got 'im in the back, stackin' crates for me," Billy answered.

"Get 'im out here. We wanna talk to 'im."

"Yeah," Tom added. "Tell 'im we'll buy him a drink, that'll bring 'im out."

A moment later a small, dispirited man shuffled out to the table. He needed a shave and his clothes reeked of stale whiskey and vomit. He studied the men around the table, then stopped when he saw Frank. Frank was someone he didn't know . . . or could it be that he *did* know him? Frank could see the struggle for recollection going on in Wyland's eyes. Wyland raised his hand to his chin. His hand was trembling badly, though whether from fright or the need of alcohol, Frank didn't know.

"Wyland, we want some information," Abner said. "If you know the answers, it'll be worth a drink."

"All right," Wyland said quietly.

"You've rode with some pretty desperate men, right?"

"I reckon I have," Wyland said.

"Who?"

"I started out with Quantrill," Wyland said. "Rode with the Reno brothers some, then took up with the James boys. Rode with Dick Liddil, too." He reached toward the table with a shaking hand. "Can I have my drink now?"

"Not yet," Frank said, reaching out to stop Wyland's hand. "We're more interested in who you been with lately," Frank said. "Three men, one tall, with a ripped ear, he's the leader of the group. Another stocky, red hair, scar over his right eyebrow. The last is a half-breed, maybe half Mexican, half Indian. He's dark, has dark hair worn in long braids. Wears a Mexican-style mustache, has a mashed nose."

Frank's descriptions were clear and concise, and the others around the table looked at him, surprised at his ability to put the question so clearly.

Frank had stared directly into Wyland's face while he asked the question, and he saw Wyland blanch. His eyes clouded over with what could only be described as fear. He took a step back from the table.

"No . . . I . . . I never heard of nobody like that," he said.

"You're lying, Wyland," Frank said matter-of-factly.

"Well now, hold on there," Abner said. "You got no call to tell a man he's lyin', just 'cause he's a drunk."

"Yeah, what makes you so sure he's lyin'?" Paul asked.

"Look at him," Frank said. "He wants it enough to make up an answer for us, and if he didn't know, that's what he'd do. But more than he's thirsty, he's scared. What are you afraid of, Wyland?"

"Nothin'," Wyland said. "I don't know who you're talkin' about, that's all."

"You know, I believe Frank's right," Abner said. "Wyland, you *do* know, don't you?"

"Don't be scared," Paul put in. "We're here."

"You're here?" Wyland said. he tried to laugh, but it came out as a weak, bark. "So you're gonna protect me if they come for me?"

"You do know them, don't you?"

"What if I do?"

"Then tell us," Tom insisted. "Tell us so we can tell the law. My God, man, have you heard what those bastards did? They killed a fifteen-year-old boy, then they raped his sister while the girl's mama and daddy had to watch. Bastards like that don't deserve to live."

"Yeah, well, when they hang, I'll stand in the crowd an' watch. But I'm not gonna do anything to help catch them."

Abner slid a bottle of whiskey toward him. "Forget about the drink, Wyland. We'll give you a whole bottle."

"Not for a case of whiskey will I tell," Wyland said.

"Wyland," Frank said quietly. "Seems to me like you're scared of the wrong people. The three men we're asking about are out there, somewhere. I'm right here in front of you. If you're gonna be scared of someone, be scared of me."

"Yeah," Tom said laughing. "Be scared of . . . ,"

the laughter died in his throat when he saw the expression on Frank's face. It wasn't one of passion, or even cold fury. He wasn't sure what he saw . . . maybe something in Frank's eyes. But he felt the hackles stand up on the back of his neck as he realized he was looking into the face of death.

"Who . . . who are you?" Wyland asked, his words barely audible.

"Frank Shaw."

The name wasn't spoken very loudly, but it stopped everyone in the room as if there had been a gunshot. The card game came to a halt, two of the men who had been talking at the bar turned around, and there was deadly silence in the room.

The clock ticked loudly.

Wyland's bottom lip began trembling and a line of spittle ran down his chin.

Frank took the badge out of his shirt pocket and pinned it on.

"Now, I'm gonna ask you again, Wyland. And I want you to think about it. And while you're thinking, I want you to know that I'm here, and they aren't."

"I . . . I knowed it was you," Wyland said.

"Start talking, Wyland," Frank said.

Wyland drew a deep breath and held his hands up. "All right, I know 'em. But I didn't have nothin' to do with them killin' that boy or rapin' the girl."

"I know you didn't," Frank said. "If you did, I would've killed you by now."

"No, sir. I didn't have nothin' at all to do with that. Sure, I rode with 'em a while when we was just stealin'. But when they commenced killin' folks, why I backed out. I ain't seen 'em since."

"Who are they? What are their names?"

"Listen, if I tell, I gotta have some money,"

Wyland said. "I gotta have enough to get out of here. My life won't be worth a plugged nickel iffen they find out I tole on 'em."

"Their names," Frank said again.

Wyland poured himself a glass of whiskey before he spoke, and this time no one attempted to stop him. He drank it, then wiped the back of his hand across his mouth.

"The tall one, the one that's the leader, his name is Shelby Priest. He's real crazy, mister, he'll kill just for the hell of it. The red haired one is Alex O'Neary. He's a wild Irishman. The breed is Hector Gitano. They say he kilt his own father. They're mean, mister. They're meaner'n sin."

"Take the bottle," Frank said.

"Thanks," Wyland said, picking it up.

"It'll keep you company in jail."

"In jail? I told you, I didn't have nothin' to do with the killin'."

"I know," Frank said. "But Marshal Remington will want to talk to you. I aim to keep you handy until I'm ready to go back, then I'm gonna take you with me."

Wyland turned the bottle up and took another long drink.

"All right," he said. "But you're responsible for me. If they come into town, you gotta protect me."

"You don't fret about that," Frank said. "That's my worry."

"Sure. My life, but your worry," Wyland said.

Frank stood up, then looked back at the table.

"Sorry about the deception, gents," he said. "Sometimes a fella can learn more if he doesn't put all his cards on the table at the same time."

"Yeah," Abner said. "Well, if you catch up with

them, it'll be worth it. Don't none of us like to see
people like that goin' around free."

"I'll do my damndest to see it don't happen,"
Frank promised.

The rain had stopped by now, so when Frank led
his prisoner down to the jail the only thing he got wet
was his feet.

"What's the charge?" the sheriff asked, when
Frank pushed Wyland in the door before him.

"No charge."

The sheriff looked around at Frank. "I can't keep
him in jail with no charge," he said. "The judge'll
let him out first thing tomorow."

"All right, say it's protective custody."

"Can't do that either, less the prisoner agrees."

"He agrees," Frank said. "Don't you?"

"I don't know," Wyland hesitated.

"You can't force him, deputy," the sheriff said.
"If he wants out, I'm going to let him out now."

"If you get out now, I'll let the word out that we
know who the three are, and how we found out,"
Frank said.

"No!" Wyland gasped.

"Then I reckon you want protective custody?"

"Yes," Wyland said.

The sheriff reached for the whiskey bottle. "Can't
have that in jail," he said.

"I say he can," Frank said quietly.

The sheriff looked at Frank, then sighed. He knew
Frank Shaw, knew the determination of the man.

"All right," he agreed. "But don't be passin' that
bottle around to any of the other prisoners."

Wyland smiled. "That's one rule I can gladly
follow," he said.

Chapter Five

Tom Beck sat with his back against a large rock, watching the flames of his fire dance and lick against the bottom of his coffee pot. His horse was cropping grass nearby. Tom knew that no prowlers could approach without the horse reacting, so he would be forewarned should there be any danger.

Tom reached for the coffeepot and poured himself a cup, then sipped the dark brew through lips that were extended to cool the drink. He chewed on a piece of beef jerky.

He had been out over a week and though he had found evidence of a few camps, he hadn't found anything that gave him a good, solid lead. Then, this afternoon, he located a corral. The droppings in the corral indicated that it had been used recently. Also, as there were oats in the droppings, he knew the horses hadn't been kept in the fields, but were boarded in a livery or a barn. They were brought here from somewhere else.

Tomorrow, he would follow the trail out of the corral to see where it led.

It led to the little town of Chetopa, Kansas. Tom rode in the next morning, his clothes well covered with the dust of travel. He made a careful study of each building in the line of false-fronted business

42

establishments that fronted the single street. He passed a pool hall, a small cafe, a saloon, a hotel, and a general store. He headed toward the store, where he intended to buy a package of horehound candy. He liked to suck on the little pieces while he was on the trail. Also, he knew from experience that a general store was a pretty good place to pick up information.

The morning sun beat down onto the dust of the street, the dried wood of the splintered walk, and the gray, whip-sawed board walls of the buildings. One beam caught the glass windowpane of the store and threw back a flash of gold.

Tom dismounted in front of the store, dusted himself off as well as he could, then went in. The interior was rich with the smells of a general store: coffee beans, stone-ground flour, and smoked meats. A pretty, brown-haired woman, about twenty-eight, was looking at dress material while her young son stood near-by, holding onto her skirt. At the back of the store a man was trying on hats.

Tom walked up to the counter then pointed to a jar of brown candy pieces. He pulled a coin from his pocket and lay it on the counter.

"Let me have a nickel's worth o' horehound," he said.

"Yes, sir. Best thing they is to cut the trail dust. Soothin' to the throat, and it's good for you besides. Ain't nothin' that'll cut the ague like horehound candy," the clerk said, as he began scooping the candy into a little cloth sack.

Tom took a couple of pieces and, securing the woman's permission, gave them to the boy. The boy thanked him and popped one into his mouth.

Tom looked back at the clerk. "I'm a deputy U.S. marshal," he identified himself. "I'm on the trail of three men. One of 'em's tall, got hisself a mangled ear, another's dark, with long braids, an' the last one is stout and red-haired. Got a scar over his eye, here." Tom made a motion over his right eye with his thumb. Ever seen anyone like that?"

The store clerk looked quickly toward the man who was trying on hats, and Tom saw a flash of fear cross his eyes. The fear told Tom that the clerk knew about the three.

Tom looked toward the man trying on hats to see why the clerk had glanced that way. The hat man didn't fit any of the descriptions, but it could be that the clerk was just frightened to say anything in front of anyone.

"No," the clerk said. "I've never heard tell of anyone like that."

The little bell on the door rang as the woman and child left the store.

"You sure?"

"Never heard of them," the clerk insisted. A line of perspiration beads spread across his upper lip.

Tom walked back to the mirror. "What about you, mister? You ever heard of these men?"

"I'm a stranger here," the man said flatly. "Just passin' through."

"Oh? Where are you from?"

"Here, there, everywhere," the man said.

"Look," Tom said in exasperation. "These here men killed a fifteen-year-old boy, last week. Didn't you hear about it? And they raped a fifteen-year-old girl while they made her mama and daddy watch. Don't you want to see people like that caught?"

"It ain't none of our concern, mister," the man with the hat said.

"What if it was you they was after? Would it be your concern then?"

"You're the law," the clerk said. "You take care of it."

Tom gave a sigh of disgust, then walked out the front door.

"Mister?" It was a woman's voice, frightened, and so quiet he could barely hear it. It came from behind the corner of the building. "Don't turn around, I don't want anyone to see me talking to you," the voice said.

"What is it?" Tom asked.

"I know you're a good man. You must be, givin' my boy candy like you done. I want to help you."

"How?"

"I heard you ask about those three men.

"They stole a horse from us three months ago. My husband followed them, saw where they went. He came back and reported it to the sheriff, but the sheriff didn't do anything."

"What happened then?"

"Nothing," the woman said. "Clyde wanted to go out and get the horse back by himself, but I wouldn't let him. They've probably sold it by now, anyway."

"Where did he find them?"

"There's a cabin, about five miles west of here," she said. "It's on a level bench by a creek, near a stand of cottonwood trees."

"Thanks," Tom said.

"Don't thank me, just find those men and arrest them. And don't tell anyone where you heard."

Tom got on his horse then. Not until he was in the middle of the street did he allow his eyes to glance at the corner of the building where the woman had been. By that time she was gone. He hoped nobody saw her there.

*   *   *

The little cabin was just where the woman said it would be, on a level piece of ground under a spread of cottonwood trees. The stream wasn't very large but it was swift-flowing, and would provide water. The cabin was well located, well built, and deserved more than to be the hideout of a gang of outlaws.

As he studied the cabin he wondered about the history of it. Surely it wasn't built by the three outlaws whose trail he was dogging. They weren't apt to take the time to build anything. More likely it was built by a couple of settlers, a man and woman with dreams of the future. What happened to them? Were they killed and their cabin taken over?

Tom stopped a quarter of a mile away from the cabin. He studied it for a long time, then, convinced that no one was there, rode up slowly. He dismounted in a stand of trees behind the cabin, reasoning that if he kept his horse out of sight there would be less chance of anyone seeing him here.

The first thing he noticed, even before he reached the cabin, was the odor. The cabin reeked of foul smells. When he reached it he saw why. The walls and corners of the cabin had been used for toilets and the smell was overpowering. Entrails, skins, feathers, and bones from game animals and birds were scattered about. Inside the cabin there were residues of food hardened to uncleaned dishes, stuck to the table and floor. The beds were filthy, the coverings soiled and stained.

Strewn about the house were signs that the men had often brought women here. He found a couple of bonnets, a carpetbag, some women's shoes, a few pieces of jewelry. One of the beds had pieces of rope tied to the head and foot and his stomach revolted as he realized that some unfortunate woman must have been a prisoner here while the men raped and tortured her.

Tom saw a kerosene lamp and he raised the chimney to check the wick, to see how long it had been since the lamp was last used. Suddenly the chimney exploded in a shower of glass as a bullet smashed through the window, beating the sound of the shot. Tom dived for the floor as a second shot sizzled through the window like an angry hornet.

Tom, his pistol in his hand, wriggled across the floor to the door. He looked outside and saw a little puff of smoke hanging above a rock. He fired at the rock, heard his bullet sing hollow and mournful as it hit the rock, then caromed off into the trees with a pinging whine.

"Hey, mister, whoever the hell you are, that there's our house," someone called from outside.

"Yeah, and we don't take kindly to strangers comin' into our house without we ask them."

There was another flurry of gunfire from outside and bullets zinged and popped through the cabin, smashing into table legs, bouncing off the stone flashing of the fireplace.

Tom fired through the door, then rolled quickly away. He was lucky he did because three bullets crashed into the door frame, chewing away big pieces of wood where his head had been just a moment before.

These men were good. And determined as hell to draw blood.

"You might as well come on out here," one of them called. "Else we'll burn you out."

"Yeah," another added laughing. "It don't bother us none to burn our own house iffen it'll catch a rat."

There was another outbreak of shots, and again

bullets probed and ricocheted through the cabin, breaking glass and splintering wood into frazzled toothpicks. A stone chip from the fireplace hit Tom in the face, and he felt a trickle of warm blood running down his cheek. Tom put his arms over his head, covering up, as the bullets whistled by. He felt as if he had stuck his head in a hornet's nest, only these hornets were deadly.

"O'Neary," one of the men outside called.

"Yeah?"

"O'Neary, you get 'round to the left there. Gitano, you go to the right. We'll get 'im in a crossfire."

Tom raised himself up to the window and saw two men running to the places they were directed. He snapped a shot off at each of them, but his shots were answered immediately by rifle fire, so accurate that he had to duck again.

Tom looked toward the back wall of the house. There was one window near the top. It was small, but then Tom Beck wasn't a large man. He smiled. If Remington was in this spot, he'd be out of luck. But Tom figured he could squeeze through the window. Barely, but he could do it.

Tom dragged the table over, climbed onto it, then pushed through the window. He had to work his way through it head first and when he came out on the other side, he would have to drop to the ground, about ten feet down. It wasn't a very pleasant prospect, but it was better than staying in the cabin and being shot or burned out.

Tom wriggled through, then tumbled down to the ground behind the cabin. He looked right and left to make certain he wasn't seen, then he ran, crouched, to the trees behind the house. The men were still shooting into the cabin, so he knew he hadn't been discovered yet.

He was glad now that he had left his horse back here.

"Hey, Priest? Priest, I think we must'a kilt him!" one of the outlaws called. "He ain't shootin' back no more."

"You wanna walk down there, go ahead," the one called Priest answered.

Tom mounted his horse, then kicked his bootheels against the sides of the animal. Unfortunately there was no way he could leave without them seeing him. He counted on surprise to help him make his getaway, and the surprise worked because all three men stood there, their guns at their sides, watching in total shock.

"What the hell? How'd the sonofabitch get out?"

"Shoot 'im! Shoot the bastard!" Priest called, suddenly realizing that his quarry was getting away. All three men raised their guns and started firing, the sounds of their shots rolling back from the hills and trees like distant thunder, empty drums.

Tom's horse galloped past the three men, with Tom bent low over the pommel, offering a small target and urging his animal to its greatest speed. He heard the bullets whip by him, and one of them clipped the brim of his hat, but in a matter of a few seconds he was away, out of range and sight.

"More black-eyed peas, Marshal Remington?"

"Thank you, Mrs. Ferrell, I believe I will," Ned said, taking the bowl from the sheriff's wife. When they reached Neosho, Ned and Russell Milsap accepted Sheriff Garland Ferrell's invitation to supper. Ned enjoyed the meal because he always enjoyed the chance to eat well when he was on the trail. It was more than enjoyment for young Milsap, though. Milsap

was so poorly equipped to live on the trail that this
meal was practically a life-saver.

"I don't think I've ever eaten this well, Mrs.
Ferrell," Milsap said.

"You're very kind, Mr. Milsap," the sheriff's
wife said. "Garland tells me you are a lawyer . . .
you went to college?"

"Yes, ma'am. Washington University in St. Louis."

"My, my, think of that. We don't often get to see
college men down here. You must be very smart."

"I wouldn't say that," Milsap replied self-con-
sciously.

"And yet you are on the trail after dangerous
criminals with Marshal Remington. You're not only
smart, you're a very brave young man, besides."

"I think foolish would be a better word," Milsap
said, and Ned laughed. Trailing had been hard on
Milsap, but the young man hadn't complained . . .
not one word. It was going to get rougher, but Ned
believed Milsap had the sand to take it. He decided
that the judge was right to send Milsap along. He
would be a better prosecutor because of it.

"Ned, how is Katy?" Mrs. Ferrell asked. "Or is it
too painful to you for me to ask?"

Ned sighed. "No, it isn't too painful, and I appreciate your interest," Ned said. "I visit her as often as
I can. She recognizes me now, and she talks some."

"Thank God for that," Mrs. Ferrell said. "I'm
sure that, with His grace, your Katy will get well
again."

"I certainly hope so," Ned said.

"What about the fella who did it?" the sheriff
wanted to know. "Passmore, was it?"

"Lucas Passmore," Ned said. "I got pretty close
to him a few weeks ago," he said. "But he got
away."

"That must've been galling."

"Yeah, it was."

"And now you're on the trail of someone entirely different."

"Different men, maybe, but they're the same type. Cockroaches that walk upright. I may not get Passmore, but I'm putting hardcases like him out of society."

"These three men you're after," Sheriff Ferrell said. "I don't know their names, but I certainly know of them."

"They've been through here, then?"

"Yes, several times. They haven't killed anyone in my county, but they've stolen stock, food, and supplies. Folks around here have heard that they've killed in other places, and they're terrified. They've been after me to do somethin', but of course, I can't do anything out of Newton County. It would just be a matter of luck if I caught them here."

"Yes," Mrs. Ferrell said. "Bad luck. I hope you don't catch them here."

"Now, Martha, that's my job," Sheriff Ferrell said. "And if I catch them here, I'm going to arrest them."

"Do me a favor if that happens, Garland," Ned said.

"What's that?"

"Don't try and do it alone."

Ferrell chuckled. "Don't worry," he said. "It's my job to arrest them if I can . . . but it isn't my job to be foolish about it. If the chance ever comes up, I'll have a whole posse behind me."

"Good."

"Where do you go next?" Ferrell wanted to know.

Ned told him about the excursions he had sent Frank Shaw and Tom Beck on. "We'll cross over into Kansas, meet up with them at Baxter Springs in a couple of days,'' he said. ''By that time I hope we have a pretty good idea as to what to do next.''

''When you bring these fellas back to hang, that's one event I want to witness,'' Ferrell said. ''That is, if you bring them back.''

''What do you mean, *if?*'' Milsap asked, looking up from the blackberry cobbler Mrs. Ferrell had just put before him.

Sheriff Ferrell lit his pipe before he answered, making quite a dramatic show of the operation.

''These three have been braggin' that they won't be taken alive. And who can blame 'em? They know they're gonna hang if they're ever brought in, so they got nothin' to lose.''

''Oh, they'll hang,'' Ned said. ''I promise you that, Garland. These three men will hang.'' He paused. His eyes narrowed. ''By the neck until dead,'' he whispered to himself with gritted teeth.

And the look in his eyes was far away and chilling as a December wind on a flat Kansas plain.

Chapter Six

There was a small apartment attached to the back of the freight office in Baxter Springs. It was built as a place to allow draymen and their shotgun guards from other towns to stay the night while waiting for loads. The room had a wood-burning cookstove, eight bunks, a dining table, and two or three well-used decks of cards.

Frank Shaw knew the owner of the freight line, so it wasn't difficult to arrange for the marshals to meet there while they planned their next move. Of course, they could've gone to the city marshal's office, but had they done so it would have gotten out that there was a convention of U.S. marshals in town. After that, any hope of surprise they may have held would be compromised.

Frank and Lou Wyland arrived in Baxter Springs first. Frank had not allowed Wyland a drink since he finished the bottle, and Wyland was going through the pains of sobering up. It was late afternoon now, and Wyland lay on one of the bunks, moaning quietly, while Frank was frying bacon for his supper.

"Please," Wyland said. "That smell is making me sick."

"Why, you're crazy," Frank said. "There's nothin' smells better'n bacon sizzlin' in the pan."

"It's killin' me," Wyland complained.

A few minutes later the door from the front office opened, and Ned and Milsap came in. Before they said anything Ned glanced over at Wyland, his glance asking the question.

"His name is Lou Wyland," Frank said. "You had your supper? Got some biscuits goin', gonna make a little pork gravy when I finish the bacon."

"Sounds good to me," Ned said. "I'm pretty sure the prosecutor would like something."

"I sure would," Russell said. "I'm getting a little tired of jerky and beans."

"Frank began cutting off more slices of bacon, laying the thick strips in the pan alongside what was already cooking. "Wyland used to ride with the men we're looking for."

"What's he told you?" Ned asked.

"So far, only their names," Frank admitted. "He's been drunk ever since I picked him up."

"Do you believe him?"

"Yeah," Frank said. "And if the sonofabitch don't up an' die on us, I think we'll get more out of 'im."

"Good," Ned said. "I'm glad you brought him along. What have you found out, so far?"

"I'll tell you what I've learned while we're eatin' supper," Frank promised.

The men were half way through their meal of biscuits, gravy and bacon, when Tom Beck arrived. Tom poured himself a cup of coffee, fixed himself a plate, and joined the others at the table.

"I seen the three of 'em," Tom said. "Fact is, I seen a hell of a lot more of 'em than I wanted to."

"Why? What happened?"

"I found some of their camps, a corral, and finally one of their cabins. While I was there they jumped me, an' damn near kilt me. Even after I got out of the cabin they chased me purt' near half-way here. I liked to not have got shed of 'em.''

"Damn," Ned said. "I wish we had been around then. We could've ended it."

Tom chuckled. "Yeah, well, as it is, they damn near ended me. How'd it go with you all?"

Frank went over again what he had told Ned and Milsap, including the names of the men they were after.

"Yeah, them names square with what the three galoots that jumped me was callin' each other," Tom said. "They was yellin' back an' forth the whole time. Never heard no first names, but the last names is just what you said."

Ned told what he and Milsap had found out, that the three men were known and feared in Newton County, but that was all.

"Why don't we ask Wyland if he knows about the cabin Mr. Beck found?" Milsap suggested.

"Good idea, Mr. Prosecutor. Why don't you ask him?" Ned invited. "That's along your line, isn't it?"

Milsap, smiling with pleasure over the fact that Ned was entrusting a critical part of the operation to him, got up from the table and walked over to the bunk.

"Mr. Wyland, my name is Russell Milsap. I'm an assistant prosecuting attorney and I'd like to ask you a few questions."

Wyland's eyes were tightly closed and he was shaking terribly. He didn't open his eyes for Milsap. In fact, he gave no indication he even heard Milsap's question.

"Mr. Wyland?"

Still no response.

Milsap put his hand down to feel Wyland's neck.

"Marshal," Milsap called out. "Marshal, you better come look at this man. I think he's dying."

Ned and the others went over to the bunk to look down at Wyland. His trembling had nearly become convulsive, his skin was leaden, and when Ned lifted one of his eyelids, Wyland's eyes were rolled way back in his head.

"Damn," Ned said. "He's dying of the delirium. Anyone got any ideas?"

"I know a Indian cure, might work," Tom suggested.

"Try it," Ned said. "We can't afford to let him die 'till we get some more information out of him."

"Well, that's the trouble with this method," Tom said.

"What do you mean?"

"It'll either cure 'im, or kill 'im, an' you never know which way it's gonna go."

Ned rubbed his chin and looked at Wyland. Finally he sighed. "Do it. He's gonna die anyway if we don't do somethin'. We might as well take the chance."

"All right. But I'm gonna need the gunpowder from about eight bullets," Tom said. "An' I'll be damned if I'm gonna give 'em all up myself. Bullets cost money."

"All right, we'll do two apiece," Ned said, sliding two .44 caliber shells from the loops of his pistol belt. He handed them to Milsap. "You take the powder out, Russell. Now, Tom, what else do you need?"

"Some cayenne pepper, a bit of quinine and coffee," Tom said. "An' a little grease . . . Frank, I reckon some of your gravy will do for that."

While Milsap extracted the gunpowder, Frank walked down to the general store to pick up the cayenne and quinine. A while later the concoction was prepared.

"Now, we'll have to give him one more drink to bring him out of the shakes and trembles," Tom said. "When he comes out of that, we gotta make him drink this whole cup."

Milsap looked at the concoction Tom had put together and wrinkled his nose.

"Glad it's him an' not me," he said.

"Don't know if a sober man could even drink this," Tom said.

"Here's a bottle of whiskey," Ned offered. "How much do I give him?"

"Better give him a whole glass. It'll take that much to bring him around."

Ned poured a glass of whiskey and handed it to Tom. Tom held it under Wyland's nose and, just as he thought it would, the smell caused Wyland to start coming around.

"Here," Tom said. "Drink this."

Wyland opened his mouth and Tom poured the whiskey in him. His throat worked automatically, gulping the liquor down. As Tom had indicated, Wyland began coming around after the whiskey. The trembling stopped and he was even able to sit up.

"Thanks," Wyland said in a hoarse voice.

"Here, I got another drink for you," Tom said, holding the concoction out to him.

Almost as a reflex action, Wyland reached for the cup. He drank about half of it before he realized what he was drinking. When he started to gag and protest, Ned forced his head back while Tom poured the rest of it down his throat. After that Wyland began retching and trembling, then he lay on his side with his knees drawn up, holding his stomach and moaning.

"It'll take a while," Tom said.

*   *   *

It took all night, but when the men woke up the next morning, they were gratified to see that Wyland was still alive. He was not only alive, he was in much better shape than he had been the night before. Though his face was still pinched and drawn, his eyes were open and clear. Wyland sat on the edge of his bunk while Frank cooked flapjacks for their breakfast. When Wyland said that he would eat some, they knew he was out of danger.

"What do you know of the cabin Tom found near Chetopa?" Ned asked over breakfast.

"It u-used to belong to a man named Hugh McCoy, an' his wife," Wyland stuttered. "Priest was tellin' in town how McCoy an' his wife went out to California an' sold the place to him. But I think he killed them."

"What makes you think that?"

"Just some of the things they said sometimes," Wyland said. "I never know'd for sure an' I never asked. I just got my suspicions 'bout it."

"You should see the cabin, Ned," Tom said. He shook his head. "It's the most filthiest thing I ever saw." Tom looked at Wyland. "I seen sign that they brought some women out there. Was you ever out there for that?"

Wyland looked down at his plate for a long moment before he answered. "That's why I left 'em," he said. "They brought a woman out from Coffeyville. She was a whore, but that didn't give 'em no license to do what they done to her. It was . . . it was awful what they done. Then, when they got through with her, they kilt her."

"And you didn't have anything to do with it?" Ned asked sharply.

"No, no, I swear I didn't," Wyland said. "Oh,

when they first brung her out there, why, I took my
turn with her. But that was early an' she was still
laughin' an' carryin' on with us. That was when she
still thought we was gonna pay her."

"You knew you wasn't gonna pay her nothin',
didn't you?" Frank asked.

"Yes, I reckon I did know that," Wyland admitted. "But I thought that was all. I thought we was
just gonna use her, then take her back to Coffeyville
and let her go. I didn't know they was gonna do the
other stuff . . . the torturin' an' all. And I didn't
know they was gonna kill her. When they done that, I
got on my horse an' left, an' I ain't seen 'em since."

"I don't believe you, Wyland," Ned snarled. "Not
for a minute. And when I get you back to Judge
Barnstall's court, you're gonna hang with the others."

"No! I'm tellin' the truth, Marshal, I swear I
am!" Wyland pleaded.

"You're gonna have to prove it."

"How? I'll do anything I have to to prove it."

"You're gonna help us catch them."

"All . . . all right. If that'll convince you. What
do you want?"

"Start out by telling me everything you know
about them," Ned ordered.

"All right." Wyland sighed. "The cabin near
Chetopa you aleady know about. They got another
one up close to Oswego."

"Where do they go for their supplies?"

"When they ain't stealin' them, you mean? They
go into Coffeyville a lot. But mostly they'll just take
what they need, from farmers if they have to. What
they really like though, is immigrants."

"Who?"

"You know, travelers. Say a man an' his family is
passin' through on a wagon. That's just like wavin' a

red flag at a bull as far as Priest is concerned. Wagons, and farms that's just got a few people livin' there, is fair game for him.''

"Tell me something about Priest."

"Priest is the leader of the bunch," Wyland said. He laughed. "I first seen 'im durin' the war. He rode with Quantrill some, but he pretty soon went out on his own. He called hisself a lieutenant, but he didn't really have no rank. I mean no rank that was give him by the guv'ment or anything. His pa is a preacher, did you know that? He says he's the way he is 'cause he wants his pa to be proud of 'im. You know how he got that ear ripped up like that?''

"How?"

"It was near 'bout bit off by that whore we took out to the cabin from Coffeyville. I reckon he was thinkin' about that when he kilt her. 'Course, he would'a kilt her anyway. He gets pleasure from killin'. I mean, the other two, they'll kill quick enough, and the killin' don't mean nothin' to 'em one way or the other. But Priest, he gets his pleasure from killin'.''

"What about the other two?" Ned wanted to know.

"The Breed has a Indian ma and a Mexican pa. He says the first man he ever kilt was his papa. Said his pa used to get drunk and beat up his ma, an' when the breed was twelve he waited 'till his pa was passed-out drunk, then he slit his throat.

"All three of 'em are dead shots with a rifle or pistol, includin' the breed, but what he really likes is a knife. He's a good knife-fighter, but what he most likes to do is just cut people up good.''

"And the Irishman?"

"He deserted from the army durin' the war," Wyland said. "He was a sergeant in the yankee army, an' he an' the four privates in his squad was supposed to take the payroll to his company com-

mander. They was near two thousand dollars in the
payroll so O'Neary decided to keep the money for
hisself. He killed them four privates and skedaddled.
Think of that . . . bein' in the war an' all, an' gettin'
kilt by your own sergeant. I always thought that was
a pretty mean thing to do.

"I used to think it was strange him an' Priest bein'
friends, seein' as Priest was a rebel and O'Neary was
a yankee. But then I got to thinkin' on it some, an' I
figured that it weren't no more'n just happenstance.
Neither one of 'em ever really cared who won the
war. They was just out for themselves."

"Whereas, you were a true patriot, right, Mr.
Wyland?" Milsap asked sarcastically.

"I was when I was ridin' for Quantrill," Wyland
insisted.

Frank rubbed his chin, then looked at the other
men around the table.

"I've chased after a lot of men," he said. "But
it's been a while since I was after anyone I wanted as
much as I want these men."

"I got good strong feelin' about it myself," Tom
said. "Anybody got 'ny ideas?"

"Why don't we go back to the cabin you found?"
Milsap asked. "Maybe we'll find them there."

"No, I don't think so," Ned said. "If they had
killed Tom, I'd say they might still be there. But
with Tom getting away, they'll be afraid that he
might tell someone about the place."

"What about the other cabin? The one Wyland
told us about in Oswego?"

"Could be we'll wind up there," Ned said. "But
I've got another idea I'd like to try first."

"What's that?" Frank asked.

"Next time they go after supplies, I want to be
there, waiting for them."

"You mean Coffeyville?"

"No, not Coffeyville. There are too many things that could go wrong if we tried to take them in Coffeyville. Innocent people standing around might get hurt."

"Then where? That's where they go for their supplies."

"Not always," Ned reminded them. "Wyland, didn't you say they'd attack a wagon if they had the chance?"

"Always," Wyland agreed.

Ned smiled. "Then we're gonna give them that chance."

Chapter Seven

"This ain't gonna work unless we got a woman along," Frank said. "They ain't gonna attack a wagon load of men."

"We're going to have a woman along," Ned said. He unwrapped a package and took out a dress and bonnet, then dropped it on the bunk. "Wyland, these clothes ought to be just about your size," he said.

"Haw!" Frank chuckled. "I hadn't thought of that."

"I ain't wearin' no women's clothes!" Wyland protested.

"Why not?" Tom asked. "They'll be the first clean clothes you've had on in over a year."

"But they's women's clothes!"

"What are you bellyachin' about?" Milsap asked. "I have to ride alongside you as if you're my wife. You know what my friends back in St. Louis would say if they thought I had taken up with somebody as ugly as you?"

"Get someone else to put on these clothes. I ain't gonna do it," Wyland said.

Ned glared at Wyland. "There is no one else," he said. "You're going to do it, if I have to put a gag in your mouth and tie you to the wagon seat."

Wyland, still swearing in anger, slipped the dress

over his clothes. "You got no right to do this," he growled.

"I don't need the right, Wyland. I've got the might," Ned said.

Russell Milsap looked over at Ned and his eyes narrowed in disapproval. "Marshal Remington, one doesn't do things, simply because one *can* do them," he said.

"You may be schooled in lawbook law, Mr. Milsap," Ned said. "But common law is a lot stronger. Might making right is common law. Now you get Wyland ready and see to it that he doesn't give us away."

Milsap's first thought was to remind Ned that, as an assistant prosecutor, he was an officer of the court, and Ned had no right to speak to him in such a manner. Milsap's second thought, and a better one, was to forget about his first thought.

"Yes, sir," Milsap agreed.

Ned knowing the habits of the outlaws, had come up with a plan. He rented horses and a covered wagon from the freight office. His idea was to let Milsap drive the wagon, while Wyland, dressed as a woman, sat alongside like the dutiful wife. Frank and Tom would be back inside the covered wagon, well armed, and safely out of sight. Ned would put on overalls and a straw hat, then ride a sway-back mare alongside the wagon. For all appearances they would be a family of farmers on their way to Coffeyville.

As the wagon rolled down the main street of Baxter Springs they didn't even garner a second look from the people who were in town. That was good, he thought. It meant that they looked exactly like what they were trying to look like.

*   *   *

They were two hours out of Baxter Springs, moving slowly along Border Road, the wagon road that ran parallel with the border into the Nations. The sun beat down warmly and Ned appeared to be dozing as he sat on the sway-backed animal. The straw hat was pulled low over his eyes, heightening the illusion.

In fact, Ned's eyes were narrowed and alert, and he was ever mindful of the pistol he had stuck down in the deep pockets of his overalls. He was inviting attack by his appearance of lazy indifference . . . indeed, was hoping such an attack would come.

Ned would like nothing better than to have Priest, O'Neary, and Gitano before him. What they did to the Nelson family made his blood boil. He was sympathetic for the young boy that was killed, but he had a special feeling for the young girl who had been raped, and left addled. No rapist would ever be safe around Ned, because all rapists he brought to justice would pay not only for their own crimes, but also for the hideous crime perpetrated against Ned's wife and daughter.

The murderer of Ned's wife, and rapist of his daughter, was still at large. Passmore's freedom haunted Ned, and every time he lay flowers upon his wife's grave he made a silent vow that someday he would catch the droop-lidded man who murdered her.

Katy, his daughter, had been left broken by the ordeal. Though a grown woman, she was child-like in her behavior. Less than child-like, for a child could laugh, enjoy the beauty of a summer day, express pleasure and displeasure. Katy could do none of that. For the first several months she spoke not a word, and gave no indication that she even recognized Ned when he came to visit her. Now, she could speak in rudimentary sentences and Ned prayed that she might truly recover someday. Still, every time he visited his daughter and watched her struggle to regain a normal life, he experienced a feeling of rage. It pained him to recall the incident in Stover when he fell for Passmore's trick of calling out his own name through the door. Ned thought of seeing the man on the ground in the alley below the hotel. He could have shot him there, would have, had the other man in the room not rushed him with a knife.

Passmore got away that time, but one day Ned would catch the man who did this to his family. And until he caught him, no rapist . . . no violator of the sanctity of a family anywhere . . . would be safe from Ned Remington. He was an avenging angel from hell, come to collect the devil's due.

It took four days by wagon to cover the nearly fifty miles from Baxter Springs to Coffeyville. They could have made the trip quite easily in two days, but Ned was in no hurry. He hoped by his plodding pace to draw the outlaws into an attack.

Nothing happened.

The streets of Coffeyville were filled with men and women going about their daily business. Coffeyville was a trade center for the surrounding agricultural area and a large number of wagons were pulled up to the stores, some loading, some unloading their goods.

Milsap drove the wagon down Eighth Street into the bright and sunny Plaza, then stopped in front of Isham's Hardware. Ned stopped alongside, then looked around the town.

"What now?" Milsap asked.

"Drive on through town, park on the other side," Ned said. "Keep Wyland inside the wagon. I don't want anyone to get too close a look at him."

"You don't want anyone to get a close look at

him," Milsap laughed. "Think about me . . . about my reputation with the ladies."

Frank laughed. "Son, how can anyone as young as you have any kind of a reputation with the ladies?"

"Things have changed, Mr. Shaw," Milsap said. "It's a lot freer between men and women nowadays, than it was when you were young."

"Oh, I don't know about that," Tom teased. "Ever'body went naked when Frank was young."

"Naked?" Milsap gasped.

"Sure. Frank's so old he was around in Adam and Eve's time," Tom said, guffawing loudly.

Ned laughed with them, then got back to business. "Tom, Frank, when you see where you leave out of the wagon without anyone seein' you, get out an' come on back to town. The three of us will separate and wander around today to see what news we can pick up."

"All right, Marshal," Tom said, all business now.

"What about me?" Wyland asked.

"What about you? You just stay out of sight."

"You mean I gotta stay in this wagon all day?" Wyland asked.

"That's what I mean."

"I can't do that," Wyland complained. "I can't stay cooped up like that."

"I can put you in jail if you want me to."

"No, no, I'd rather stay with the wagon than set in a damned jail. Say, uh, Marshal, could you maybe bring me a little whiskey?"

"Can't afford to have you drunk again," Ned said.

"I was thinkin' maybe just a little would help pass the time."

"You almost d   of the williwaws." Milsap scolded. "I'd think that'd be enough." Milsap clucked to his team and the wagon started up again. Ned dismounted, and went into Isham's Hardware store.

"Yes, sir," the store clerk greeted Ned. "What can I do for you"

"I need a little information," Ned said.

The clerk smiled and held up his finger. "Don't tell me you're not a buyer."

"What?"

"I don't get a dime to answer questions," said the clerk.

"Maybe not," said Ned, "but I've got my family in a wagon just out of town. We're movin' through this part of the country and I've heard there was a gang of outlaws sometimes preyed on wagons."

The clerk's eyes narrowed slightly, then he looked around to see who was close enough to overhear him.

"Yes, sir, you got a right to be worried," he said. "They's three of the meanest critters you ever thought about out there, an' they ain't nothin' they like better'n jumpin' a farmer an' his family. An' it don't make no never mind iffen it be a wagon or at the farmer's house."

"I was afraid of that," Ned said, still playing the role. "What's the safest way to go?"

"They do most of their raidin' between here an' the Missouri line. So if you're goin' back east, you're in for it."

"I'm afraid that's the way we're going," Ned said.

The clerk scratched his head. "Well, sir, that bein' the case, my advice would be to avoid the prairie trail. Stay up on the border road much as you can."

"Thanks," Ned said. They had come by the border road and nothing happened. He would go back by the very road the clerk told him to avoid.

*   *   *

Later that day, across the street from the hardware store, and two blocks to the east, a wagon sat in front of McKenna's Livery Stable. Two young girls, one fifteen and one sixteen, sat in the back of the wagon, wedged in between boxes of clothing, a few items of furniture, household goods, a plow, and several more farming utensils. The youngest girl was Holly. The older, Clara. The girls' mother, June, sat on the seat in front while Seth Moberly, their father, was talking to Burt McKenna, the stable owner.

"If you ask me, Seth, your best bet would be to wait until Parkinson has two or three freight wagons ready for Joplin. You could follow along behind them and they'd be good protection."

Moberly pulled at his beard. "That's a good idea, Burt, an' don't think I hadn't thought of it. But Parkinson's not sendin' any more wagons 'till next week. If I'm gonna take possession of that farm, I gotta be in Joplin in five days."

"Well you keep a sharp eye out," McKenna warned.

Seth smiled, and shook McKenna's hand. "You can believe I'll do that," he said. "and I want you to know that you've been a good friend for my time in Kansas. I'll miss you."

"But you're anxious to get back to Missouri," McKenna said, smiling back at him.

"You know what they say. Once you get Missouri sand in your shoes, you'll always come back. I was borned over in Jasper County, reckon I'll die over there."

"Goodby, Seth. Good luck to you," Burt called.

Seth climbed onto the wagon and clucked at his team. As they rolled out of town Holly and Clara waved at all their friends.

"I don't know why we have to go to Missouri,

anyway,'' Holly said. ''There's probably not anyone our age in the whole county.''

''Probably not in the whole state,'' Clara added.

Seth chuckled. ''Well it would sure be a strange place if you were the only young people in the whole state.''

''Papa, you grew up in Missouri. Were there any young people there when you were young?''

''What do you think I was?''

''A boy,'' Holly pouted.

This time June laughed. ''There will come a time, daughters, when you'll be glad there are boys your age.''

''But not too soon, I hope,'' Seth said. Seth looked ahead of them and saw a wagon going in the same direction they were. However, the wagon seemed headed for the prairie trail.

''Seth, if they're going as far as Missouri, maybe we could go along with them,'' June proposed.

''Yes,'' Seth said. ''It looks like they're goin' the prairie trail, though. Maybe they don't know.''

Seth hurried the team up to a trot so that they closed the distance with the other wagon. He pulled up even with them, and when the driver looked over he touched the brim of his hat.

''Howdy,'' he called out. ''You goin' very far in this direction?''

''To Missouri,'' the driver said. The driver looked younger than the woman who was sitting beside him.

''We're going' that way too,'' Seth replied. ''It'd be good for us to go together . . . keep each other company.''

''Ask him,'' the driver said, pointing to a mounted rider who had been riding ahead, but was now coming back to join up with the wagon.

''Good day to you, sir. My name is Seth Moberly,

this is my wife, June, my two daughters, Holly and Clara. We're heading for Jasper County, Missouri. We thought it would be nice if our two wagons went together.''

"I don't know . . . we're pretty much of a private group."

Seth saw two men riding in back of the wagon. Counting the rider and driver, that made four men, besides himself. It would take a pretty bold gang of outlaws to jump five armed men. That made him all the more determined to press the issue.

"We've no wish to interfere with your privacy, sir," Seth said. "It's just that there's been trouble befallin' lone wagons travelin' out here of late. But with the two of us together, why I reckon we'd be 'bout as safe as sittin' in the middle of the Plaza. Besides, there are four men with your group, I have only myself, my wife, and two daughters. I'm askin' you as a kindness, to let us ride along with you."

"All right," the rider finally said. "You can trail along behind."

"Thank you," Seth said. "Oh, and I notice you are heading for the prairie trail. That's the most dangerous route. We'd be better off goin' by Border Road."

"The prairie trail is a day faster."

"But Border Road is much safer."

"You can go that way if you wish. We're going by the prairie trail."

"No, no, that's quite all right," Seth said. "We'll go whatever way you wish. After all, with five of us, there shouldn't be any danger."

Seth slowed his horses to allow the other wagon to get ahead, then he pulled in behind.

"I feel much better now," June said. "Though I

wish you could have talked them into going the Border Road.''

Seth chuckled.

''What is it?''

''Maybe they can't stand to travel that long with that woman. Did you see how ugly she is? I've never seen such a homely woman.''

''Seth, you're awful,'' June scolded, but both girls laughed.

Ned rode in front of the wagon. He almost told the Moberlys they couldn't ride along with him. He figured it wouldn't be right to expose them to the danger. Then he thought that they would probably be in more danger by themselves than they would be by coming along with him. And as the Moberlys really were farmers, it made his little ruse look all the more real.

He had a feeling he would hear from Priest and the others this time.

Chapter Eight

The Moberly wagon was open, with a tarp across the top for shade. The two Moberly girls were bright, bubbly, and full of life as young people are, and Ned enjoyed watching them. Sometimes they would break out in song, other times they would jump down from the wagon and dart out to one side or the other to collect wild flowers. Sometimes they would sit on the edge of the wagon, other times they would roll the tarp back and stand with their heads and shoulders above the bows, looking out across the prairie.

Holly, the youngest, was having trouble keeping her hair pinned up, and her mother had to fix it for her two or three times. Ned felt a pang of nostalgia at that, remembering the many times he had watched his own wife put up his daughter's hair.

They didn't stop for lunch, but they did stop for supper. June asked if they would like to pool their provisions and fix supper together, but Wyland, pulling his bonnet across his face, didn't answer.

"She's been ill," Ned apologized, without going any further. "Frank does most of our cooking, he'll be glad to pitch in."

"You're most welcome," June said.

"Are you a good cook, Mr. Shaw?" Holly asked.

"I've cooked a few meals in my day," Frank said.

Holly laughed. "It seems funny to see a man

cooking," she said. "I thought only women could cook."

"What makes you think that?" Frank asked. "Who do you think cooks for the cowboys when they're pushin' a herd? What about the army? Men have to cook for the army. And I have a friend, Dan Norling, who's cooked for kings and queens."

"Really?" Holly asked. "Can you cook as good as he can?"

Frank chuckled. "Not if we're in some fancy kitchen somewhere," he said. "But truth is, on the trail, why I reckon I'm about as good. See if you don't like my fried apple pies tonight."

"I'll like it," Holly said. "I like any kind of apple pie."

Between the two wagons they came up with a pot of beans cooked with smoked ham, some cornbread, and Frank's fried apple pies.

"These are the best fried apple pies I've ever tasted," Holly exclaimed.

"Holly, Mama makes good apple pies too," Clara reminded her. "How do you think it makes her feel to hear you say that?"

"Oh, Mama, I'm sorry," Holly said quickly. "Yours are good too."

June laughed softly. "You're just afraid I won't make any more for you," she said. "Don't worry, darlin', I'll still make them, though I agree with you, Mr. Shaw's fried apple pies are delicious."

"Mr. Remington, have you ever been to Missouri?" Holly asked.

"Lots of times."

"Are there any people our age in Missouri?"

"There are lots of people your age."

"I hope so," Holly said.

June sighed. "You'll have to forgive the girls," she said. "I'm afraid they would rather not move."

"I guess moving is a pretty big thing for young girls," Ned said.

"Do you have a daughter, Mr. Remington?" Holly asked.

Ned broke a stick and tossed it into the fire. "Yes," he said quietly. "I have a daughter."

June, recognizing from the tone of his voice that there was something painful about it, nudged Seth to change the subject.

"Uh, the reason we're going to Missouri is my Uncle wrote me of a piece of land that is available at a very good price," Seth said. "But I must get there quickly to take advantage of it."

"I think you'll love Missouri," Ned said to the two girls. "It's a fine place."

"Mr. Remington, don't take me wrong," Seth said. "But you don't seem like no farmer I've ever seen before."

"Why not?"

"Well, for one thing, Your cook an' hired hand are both wearing guns."

"We were told there are outlaws preying on wagons in this part of the country," Frank said.

"Yes, sir, that's true," Seth said. "And I've got me a Winchester under the seat of my wagon. It's only good sense to carry a gun when you're ridin' this trail, but you men are carryin' them in holsters. I can't see goin' to the expense of buyin' a holster rig, just to make this journey."

"Well, I guess you got my cousins pegged," Ned said easily. "They both did some cowboyin' down in Texas. I reckon they got into the habit down there."

*   *   *

Wyland had not left the wagon to join the others for supper. He was sitting up on the seat, back in the shadows, eating a plate of beans. He could see the others, and hear their conversation, but he didn't become a part of it. Ned had told him to stay out of the way, lest he be discovered. But, even if Ned had not so ordered it, he would have kept away from the others.

Wyland was growing increasingly more nervous. Part of it was the continuing need for a drink. Marshal Remington had cut him off cold, and he hadn't had a drink since Frank found him. He wanted a drink now, more than he had ever wanted one in his life.

But it wasn't just a lack of alcohol that contributed to his nervousness. Wyland was concerned about Priest, O'Neary, and Gitano. He knew that the chances were very good that they would attack this little party of travelers. If they did, and if they recognized him, his life wouldn't be worth a Confederate dollar. If he could sneak away from everyone tonight, he would do it. The trouble is, Remington was sure to set guards.

Ned and Tom Beck took the first watch. The night passed with only the sound of frogs, insects, and birds to measure the lengthening hours. Milsap and Frank relieved them at midnight, and Ned crawled under the wagon to go to sleep.

"Mr. Shaw?" Milsap called quietly.

"Yeah."

"How much longer until dawn?"

Frank looked up at the stars. "I make it another half hour or so."

"You think maybe we ought to build up the fire so we can fix coffee?"

Frank stretched, then looked over at the glowing coals of last night's campfire.

"Prob'ly wouldn't hurt anything," he said. "You toss some wood on, I'll get the coffee."

"We burned the last stick," Milsap said. "I'm gonna have to gather some more. I saw a dead limb on the ground under that tree over there. I'll go back there for some."

Frank watched the young prosecutor walk out into the dark. Though the night was clear and full of stars, there was no moon, so Milsap didn't go more than thirty yards before he disappeared.

Frank took the coffee pot over to the wagon, tossed out the dregs of last night's grounds, then took a handful of beans from a sack and put them in a small coffee grinder. He ground up fresh coffee and put it in the pot, filled the pot with water, and started back toward the fire. He saw Milsap returning with an armload of wood. He chuckled.

"Boy, how much wood do you think we need? You got enough there to . . . ," suddenly Frank stopped in mid-sentence. *The man holding the wood wasn't Russell Milsap.*

"Good mornin'," the man rasped.

"You'd be Priest?" Frank asked calmly.

"Yeah. Your friend's laying out under the tree back there with a knot on the back of his head. Turn around. Slow."

Frank turned as he was directed, then felt an excruciating pain as Priest brought his gun down on Frank's head. Frank went down.

After Priest knocked the guard out, he signalled for the other two to come in. They drifted in quickly, silently, from the darkness around the wagons.

"What we got here?" O'Neary asked.

"Couple of farmer's wagons," Priest said. He pointed to the wagon Ned had rented. "Don't look like there's nothin' in that one. Let's take a look at the other'n.''

The three men moved quietly to the Moberly wagon, then started looking through it. Gitano found a piece of cornbread left over from last night's supper and he started eating it. Quietly, they moved clothes and blankets, sticking their hands in between the folds, looking for a secret cache.

"Find anythin'?" Priest asked quietly.

"No. Hell, they ain't nothin' worth takin'," O'Neary hissed.

"What about them?" Priest asked, pointing to the two girls who were sleeping on a canvas blanket just behind the wagon.

"Yeah," O'Neary said, rubbing himself. "Yeah, they'll do just fine."

"All right, let's take 'em."

Silently, Gitano reached down for one, while O'Neary reached for the other. They grabbed both girls at the same instant, and though they put their hands over the girls' mouths, Holly managed to cry out a brief call of alarm.

"Holly?" June called, reacting immediately, alerted as only a mother can be, to her child's cry in the night. She sat up and saw her two daughters being dragged off. "Seth! My God, they have the girls!" she screamed.

"Shut up!" Priest yelled, bringing the back of his hand across June's mouth. She went down, spitting out a tooth from the blow. A second blow knocked her out.

Seth jumped up and started for the wagon and his Winchester, but Priest brought the butt of his pistol down on Seth's head. Seth went down, and Priest dropped on one knee to smash him a second time.

"Let's go!" Priest called.

The commotion woke Ned, and he sat up just in time to see Seth go down.

"Tom! Tom, we're bein' hit!"

"Where's Frank?"

"I don't know," Ned said. Ned's pistol was nearby and he reached for it, though it was so dark he could barely see what was going on. By the time he made out the shapes of the bushwhackers, he saw, also, that the men had the two girls captive.

"Watch your fire," Ned cautioned. "They've got the girls."

Ned and Frank both fired, though they hoped to startle the outlaws more than anything else. They couldn't actually shoot at them, for fear of hitting the girls.

The outlaws fired back, and they were under no such constraints. The bullets hit the wagon and sent a shower of splinters raining down on the two men underneath.

Ned fired again, the flame pattern from his pistol lighting up the night.

"Papa! Papa, help me!" one of the girls called, getting her mouth free just long enough to send out the heart-rending plea.

Ned ran barefooted across rocks and sandspurs to try and get in position to get off a good shot. It didn't help.

The three outlaws and the two girls disappeared into the night, and seconds later, Ned heard the sound of pounding hooves. They were getting away, and except for the sway-backed mare, Ned had no saddle horses to use to go after them.

"What is it?" Wyland called. "What happened?"

"Priest and his men," Ned said bitterly. "They just hit us."

"I . . . I could've been killed!" Wyland said.

"You were supposed to protect me! You promised you would protect me!"

"Shut up!" Ned growled. "You aren't hurt, and we have some people who are."

Frank came to then, and he walked toward them, rubbing the back of his head.

"I'm sorry, Ned," he apologized. "He got the drop on me. I thought it was Milsap."

"Where is Milsap?" Ned asked.

"I'm here," a voice called from the darkness. "I'm comin' in."

Milsap came in then, like Frank, rubbing his head.

"They were out there behind the tree," Milsap explained. "When I started to gather the wood one of them hit me."

"What about the Moberlys? Are they dead?"

"I don't know," Ned said. "But the girls are gone."

The sun was up by the time Seth Moberly was fully conscious. He was sitting on the ground with his back against the wagon wheel, drinking a cup of the coffee that was finally brewed. One of his eyes was swollen nearly shut. June Moberly's lip was badly swollen, her cheek bruised. She was sobbing quietly.

Wyland came down from the wagon to pour himself a cup of coffee. He wasn't wearing the bonnet, and it was clear that he was a man. Seth was surprised when he saw him.

"What . . . what is this?" he asked. "Why is he dressed like a woman?"

"Can I get out of this fool outfit now, Marshal?" Wyland asked.

"Might as well," Ned said.

"Marshal? Did he call you marshal?"

"Yes," Ned answered. He sighed, then slipped out of the coveralls he had been wearing. His regular clothes were underneath. He walked over to the wagon and fished out his holster, then strapped it on.

"What's going on here? I don't understand," Seth said.

"I'm United States Marshal Ned Remington. This is Russell Milsap, assistant prosecuting attorney for the Federal Court in Stone County, Missouri. These are my deputies, Tom Beck and Frank Shaw. This is Lou Wyland. Mr. Wyland once rode with Priest and his men, and has consented to help us find him."

"I didn't consent," Wyland complained. "You forced me into it."

June looked up at Ned with anger snapping behind the tears in her eyes. "Seems to me like we are in the same boat," she said.

"What do you mean?" Seth asked.

"We were forced into helping him as well. We were decoys, weren't we, Marshal?"

"Wait a minute," Seth said. He ran his hand through his hair. "Now I know why you insisted on coming across the prairie instead of going down Border Road. You *wanted* Priest to attack us, didn't you? You *planned* all this."

"Not entirely," Ned said. "I didn't plan for you to get hurt, or the girls to get kidnapped."

"How dare you use us like that?" Seth said. "You had no right."

"Look," Ned explained. "I'm sorry about what happened. I'd give anything in the world if your girls hadn't been caught up in this. But, if you remember, I didn't invite you along. You invited yourself. Anyway, they would have hit you with, or without us. They've become like mad men. They can't be satisfied, they'll keep on going until they're stopped."

Seth was quiet for a long moment, then he sighed.

"You're probably right," he said. "They would've hit us with, or without you. And without you, we would probably all be dead now."

"I'm glad you understand," Ned said. "And I'm sorry it happened."

"What happens now?" Seth wanted to know.

"We're going after them," Ned said. "Soon as we can get into Chetopa and get horses."

"I want to go with you."

"No," Ned said. "The best thing you can do is get your wife on safely to Joplin."

"But I want to help."

"Mr. Moberly," Ned said. "I hate telling you this, but you may as well face up to it. These men . . . they're not like normal men. The chances are that your girls are already. . . ."

"Dead?" June asked.

"Yes," Ned said.

June swallowed hard and tears streamed down her face. "It might be better for them if they are," she said quietly. June got up then, and started breaking camp. Ned and his deputies helped, and a few minutes later, the Moberly wagon started its sad, lonely trip to Joplin.

It was an hour and a half before Ned and the others were freshly mounted, riding out of Chetopa, on the trail of the outlaws. Tom Beck had fresh tracks to follow, and he was riding point. Frank Shaw rode swing, while Milsap had the responsibility for Wyland. Ned rode so he could cover Beck. There was a grim cast to his face, a hard line to his jaw. Not since his crusade to bring in Lucas Passmore, had he been more determined to bring outlaws to justice.

Chapter Nine

Priest, O'Neary, and Gitano rode south, down into the Nations. Priest intended to make a wide swing, throwing off anyone who might be tracking him. Priest looked over at the two girls, one riding in front of O'Neary, the other in front of Gitano. Both girls were tied and gagged, but their eyes were wide, and full of fear.

It was the fear, Priest believed, that he craved as much as anything. The sex was satisfying, maybe even enjoyable. But what he really liked more than anything else, was seeing the fear in the girls' eyes.

Sometimes he would kill them, and watch the fear fade as life left their eyes. Sometimes he would leave them alive and watch as the fear drove them mad. There was no rhyme nor reason as to whether he killed them or left them alive. It was just a game he played, a game he had been playing since the days he rode as a border-raider during the war.

He thought back to those days, so long ago.

He squatted on his haunches and tossed another branch onto the fire. Beyond the flickering flames shadows came and went as his men, one by one, took their turns with the young girl they had captured earlier in the day. Priest, of course, had been first. It was his right as the colonel.

Priest had appointed himself colonel, just as he had appointed himself captain when he first formed the group. He would have appointed himself colonel at the beginning, but his ignorance of military rank was such that he thought a captain was higher than a colonel. Not until later did he realize his foolish error.

Of course, as his "command" had no official recognition, he could choose any rank he wanted. He had created his own army and designated the men in his army by whichever rank he chose. He was the only officer, because he wasn't sure which rank the other officers would be, and he didn't want to take the chance of appointing someone to a higher ranking than he held himself. His second-in-command he made a sergeant.

"Sergeant" O'Neary walked over to him, buttoning up his pants. He had just left the young girl for the second time.

"You gonna visit her again, Priest?" O'Neary asked.

"I reckon I will," Priest said.

"Gitano's with her now."

"That's all right. I'm a patient man."

"You really believe what ever'one's a' sayin' 'bout Lee surrenderin'?" O'Neary asked.

"Last two or three times we've raided a town, that's what they was tellin' us," Priest said. "I reckon we've heard it enough times now that I believe it to be a fact."

"That mean the war's over?"

"I reckon it does."

"That's too bad," O'Neary said. He took a drink of whiskey, then wiped the back of his hand across his mouth. "I hate to see ole' Gen'rul Lee give up to the Yankees like that."

"What do you care whether Lee surrendered or not?" Priest asked. "We wasn't Confederates."

"We wasn't?"

"No."

"I'll be damned. Was we Yankees?"

"No, we wasn't Yankees neither."

"Well now, hell, if we wasn't Confederates and we wasn't Yankees, just what the hell was we?"

Priest chuckled. "I never quite got it figured out what we was, so I reckon we was whatever we wanted to be."

"I'll be damned," O'Neary said. He laughed. "Anyhow, that wasn't what I meant when I said too bad. I meant it was too bad the war was over. I ain't never had it as good as we've had it the last couple years, takin' what we want whenever we want it, be it horses, or food, or women."

Priest reached for the bottle then took a long swallow before he answered.

"I tell you what I been studyin' on," he finally said. "Seein' as how we never was really in this war anyhow, why do we have to stop doin' what we're doin'?"

O'Neary looked at him with a curious expression on his face. "What do you mean? You mean for us to just go on raidin' like as if the war was still goin'?"

"Why not?" Priest asked. "Like you said, we ain't never had it so good before."

O'Neary smiled broadly, then let out a whoop.

"I like that," he said. "Yes, sir, I like that a lot. Wait'll I tell the boys."

"No," Priest warned, holding out his hand. O'Neary looked back at him, questioningly. "Just tell Gitano," he said. "There's only room for the three of us."

Off and on over the past several years there had

been others come and go with Priest, O'Neary, and Gitano. But no one stayed for too long a time, so that the three men formed a bond between them that seemed as if it would never break.

There were generally two types of men to join with the group; those who joined with the idea that they could steal a lot of money and get rich . . . and those who joined for the adventure.

The ones who joined for the money soon learned that there was very little profit involved with such an operation. Priest seldom planned his jobs in advance. If they needed food, they would steal food, it they needed horses, they would steal horses. They managed to steal actual cash only rarely, and when they did, it was almost always an accident.

Those who joined for the adventure soon lost their taste for it when they discovered that the "adventure" normally consisted of hiding out in filthy cabins, riding to avoid capture, and killing and raping just for the pleasure. Killing and raping didn't appeal to many men, even those hardened by the outlaw trail. So with little money, and no adventure, Priest's little outlaw band was normally restricted to the three who originally started it.

There was only one man who ever joined their group who would have fit right in with them except for one thing. His name was Lucas Passmore, and he, like Priest, had been the leader of a group of border-raiders. As long as the two of them were together, there was always the problem of who would lead. Since this was Priest's group in the first place, Priest was the leader but everyone knew it would come to a head if they didn't separate. Finally Passmore rode off on his own.

Just before Passmore left, he and Priest were out scouting the countryside for a place to rob, when they happened onto a house where only a woman and her daughter were home. Never one to pass up an opportunity, they moved in on them.

They took turns with the mother until Passmore got tired of her and cut her throat. Then they took turns with the young girl. When the young girl passed out, Priest started to kill her, but Passmore stopped him.

"No, I want to leave her alive," Passmore said. "I want her papa to think about it ever'time he sees her."

Passmore took his knife and scratched his last name onto the polished surface of the dining-room table.

"Why'd you do that?" Priest wanted to know.

"It's gonna bother him all the more to know I was the one that done it," Passmore said. "Can you see that farmer comin' back here, seein' my name scratched on the table, seein' his woman kilt, his daughter raped? He's gonna go take his old rifle out of the closet an' come after me." Passmore giggled. "And when he does I'm gonna gut-shoot him and let him take two days to die."

"I ain't plannin' on leavin' my name."

Passmore looked at him through his ugly, drooping, eyelid.

"Don't worry, I ain't plannin' on lettin' you leave your name. This here'n is all mine."

Priest learned later that it wasn't some farmer's wife Passmore had killed. It was the wife and daughter of Ned Remington, a U.S. marshal. The marshal hadn't caught up with Passmore yet, but Priest figured that some day he would. He was glad the marshal didn't know about him and wasn't on his trail.

*   *   *

"Hey, Priest," O'Neary said, interrupting Priest's thoughts of the past. Priest looked over toward O'Neary, and saw that he had his arm around the captive girl, his hand roughly cupped over her breast.

"What do you want?"

"What say we stop for a while? They ain't no way anyone's gonna follow us down here. Hell, we been runnin' over solid rock for near 'bout an hour."

"Let me take a look-see," Priest said. He halted them, then climbed up onto a nearby hill, holding a spyglass in his hand. He opened up the telescope and looked back over the way they came. For as far as he could look, he saw nobody. He snapped the glass closed, then came back down the hill.

"Did you see anyone?" O'Neary asked.

"No."

"Then we can stop a while?"

"Yeah, all right," Priest agreed. "We'll take a little rest here, then start doublin' back. I don't want to get too far down into the Nations."

"Good," O'Neary said, getting down from his horse. He reached up and pulled the girl down. "Come on, honey, me an' you's gonna have us a little fun."

Clara's eyes opened wide in fear, and she looked at Priest, as if pleading with him, the leader, to say something.

"You gonna be wantin' a little of the fun after I get finished, Priest?" O'Neary asked.

Priest had already resolved not to do anything until they reached the cabin. But when he looked at Clara and saw her eyes wide in fear, he grew immediately excited.

"You askin' the wrong question, O'Neary," Priest said, rubbing himself. "What you mean is, do I wanna let you have some of the fun after I get finished."

"Damn!" O'Neary swore. "I thought you said I was gonna be first this time."

"I'll save some for you," Priest said, starting for the girl.

Tom Beck studied the ground for a long time. He found a scar on the ground, then a tiny, crushed pebble, a broken twig, and finally a horse dropping. They were still on the trail.

" 'Pears like they're goin' way down into the Nations," Frank said. Frank uncorked his canteen and took a long pull, then corked it and hooked it back on the pommel.

"Yeah," Ned said. "The question is, why?" Ned looked over at Wyland. "You got anything to say about this?"

"I know they like to come down here a lot to hide out and rape their women captives," Wyland offered.

"I never thought they'd go so far though," Ned said. "They've always stayed close to the border so they could move up into Missouri or Kansas, pull off their dirty work, then skip back down into the Nations. Why are they going so far this time?"

"Maybe they've never been chased before," Milsap suggested.

"What makes them think they're being chased this time?" Ned wanted to know. "For all they know, we were just farmers."

"That's a point, all right," Frank said. "But all the sign says they're goin' deep into the Nations, so we gotta figure that's where they are, whatever the reason."

"I agree with you there," Ned said. "I wish I had an idea as to where they're likely to go. We could head straight for there."

"I know where they might me," Wyland offered.

"Where?"

"They's a cave on the bank of the Neosho River," Wyland said. "Gitano pointed it out to me, told me it was a good place to hide-out. I reckon they could be goin' there."

"Did you ever go there when you were riding with them?" Milsap asked.

"No, never did. But they never done nothin' this bad when I was with them. We never done nothin' more'n a little robbin' here an' there. We didn't need no real hide-out like the cave. If you ask me, the cave's where you'll find them."

"All right, let's go to the cave," Ned said. "We'll head east to the river, then go right down the bank. That way, we might cut their trail, or run across them, just in case they double back or ride in another direction," Ned suggested.

"What if . . ." Milsap started, then he let the words die.

"What?"

"I was just thinking, what if they don't head for the river? We'll be out on a wild goose chase."

"Could be," Ned said. "But seems to me like it's a chance we gotta take."

The breed got up from Clara, then pulled his pants up. Clara, naked from the waist down, her legs spread and spotted with blood, lay on the ground. Her eyes, wide with fear when the ordeal started, were now glazed over, and though they were open, it was as if she was seeing nothing. Holly, who hadn't been touched yet, was tied to a tree nearby. Holly tried to get Clara's attention, to look at her and exchange a look of support, but when Clara looked toward her, it was as if she didn't even know her.

"What about the little one?" O'Neary asked. "We gonna take care of her too?"

"Not yet," Priest said. "Let's save her for later."

"Yeah," O'Neary said, chuckling obscenely. "We'll save her for dessert."

"You finished, Gitano?"

"Yes," Gitano answered. He finished buttoning his pants.

"Get her trussed up again," Priest said. "Let's shake a leg. I wanna get back to the cabin before dark. We're gonna start doublin' back, now."

"Still don't think they's anybody after us, do you?" O'Neary asked.

"I had me a look-see just a moment ago," Priest said. "Didn't see hide nor hair of anyone followin' us."

"We missed 'em, Ned," Tom said. The five men were standing at the mouth of the cave Wyland had told them about. There was no sign that anyone had been at the cave in months, and during their ride downriver, they had not come upon a camp, nor even cut a fresh trail.

"Damn!" Ned swore. He took off his hat and ran his hand through his hair. "I guessed wrong."

"Ever'body makes a mistake ever' now an' again," Frank suggested.

"Yeah," Ned said. "But my mistake might have cost those two girls their lives."

"No, sir," Tom said. "Your mistake don't have nothin' to do with it. If them fellas is of a mind to kill them little girls, they'll do it, no matter whether we're lookin' on at 'em or not."

"Surely that's not true," Milsap suggested. "Surely if we find them in time, we'll be able to rescue the girls."

Frank looked at Wyland. "He don't think so," Frank said. "And he knows 'em."

"Is what Mr. Beck says true?" Milsap asked. "Would they kill the girls, knowing we were right there?"

"That wouldn't stop 'em," Wyland said.

"Boss, you ready for one more guess?" Tom asked.

"Might as well be. We don't have anything left but guesses," Ned answered.

"I'm thinkin' they went back to the little cabin I found near Chetopa."

"No, they wouldn't go there," Wyland said. "They might go to the one near Oswego."

"Why do you say that?" Ned asked.

"The cabin up near Oswego is bigger and better supplied," Wyland said. "An' don't forget, they found someone in the cabin at Chetopa."

"They didn't know I was law," Tom said. "For all they know I was just a drifter, tryin' to steal their goods. And Chetopa is closer. They've got a couple of kidnapped girls with them. I don't think they're gonna wanna drag the girls around any more'n they have to."

"Go to Chetopa if you want to miss them again. I'm tellin' you they would be more likely to go to Oswego," Wyland insisted.

"What's it gonna be, Ned?" Frank asked.

"Damn. I'm inclined to agree with Tom. But Wyland know them . . . maybe he's right on this one."

"Marshal?" Milsap spoke.

"Yes."

"I know I haven't been much help to you during this trip. I got myself knocked out while I was standing guard."

"Boy, that happened to me too," Frank reminded him. "Don't go blaming yourself for that."

"Nevertheless, it happened," Milsap said. "So, like I say, I haven't been too much help so far. But that's because my training hasn't covered long manhunts." Milsap looked at Wyland. "My training *has* taught me to tell whether or not a man is lying on the witness stand, however. And this man is lying." He pointed to Wyland.

"What?" Wyland sputtered. "Why would I want to do a thing like that?"

"Why? Because you don't want us to find them."

"You're wrong, mister. I got no love for Priest and the others."

"No, but you do have an inordinate fear of them."

"A what kinda fear?" Frank asked.

"A lot of fear," Milsap simplified. "So much fear that I believe he lied about the cave just to keep us from running across Priest. And I believe he is lying now for the same reason. He doesn't want us to find Priest because he is afraid of him."

Ned studied Wyland for a long moment, saw the beads of perspiration break out on Wyland's upper lip, saw his chin tremble, his eyes dart back and forth beadily.

"Mr. Prosecutor, your objection is sustained," he said. "Come on, we're going to the cabin at Chetopa."

Chapter Ten

It grew dark an hour after Ned and his group left the cave but except for a cold camp long enough to eat some jerky and take a leak, the marshals didn't stop.

Wyland didn't quit complaining. He said he was tired, he said it was foolish to keep on in the dark because a horse could stumble and he could break his neck. Then, when a light drizzle of rain started just after midnight, Wyland complained about that.

"Wyland, if you don't shut up I'm goin' to put a bullet in your carcass and just leave you here," Tom told him.

"You won't do that," Wyland said. "You can't do that."

"Try me," Tom said coldly, and the tone of his voice frightened Wyland even more.

"Marshal, would you let him do that?" Wyland asked.

"The only way I'd stop him is if I did it first," Ned said.

"Milsap, you're a lawyer, you see how they're treatin' me. When we get back, I want you to tell the judge how these men was treatin' me," Wyland said.

"Wyland, if you don't shut up, *I'll* put a bullet in you," Milsap said.

Being censured by the youngest and most inexperi-

enced trail hand seemed to shame Wyland into silence, and for several minutes there was only the
sound of the rain and the sloshing of horses' hooves.

"Marshal Remington?" Milsap said.

"Yeah."

"Do you think we have any chance at all of saving
the girls?"

"I don't know," Ned said. "I wouldn't want to
get our hopes up."

"They were such pretty little things," Milsap said.
"And frisky as puppies. It . . . it would be a prime
shame if those men did anything to them."

"You can't dwell on that, boy," Ned said gently.
"If you do, it'll drive you crazy."

The men rode on through the night until, just
before dawn, Tom stopped them. He came back to
Ned. "It's there," he said. "Just on the other side of
the creek."

"Are they here?"

"Yeah," Tom said quietly. "They're here. Look."

Tom pointed to a lean-to alongside the cabin and
there, in the lean-to, Ned could see three horses. He
let out an audible breath.

"All right," he said. "Get the others up here."

A few moments later, Ned talked to the four men
who were with him.

"These sonsofbitches aren't going to get away,"
he said. "Do you understand that? No matter what
happens, they aren't going to get away."

"You don't know what kind of tricks they'll have
up their sleeve," Wyland warned. "Priest is a slick
one."

"Priest is a murdering, raping, low-down sonofabitch," Ned said. "And all the tricks in the world
won't help him. He won't get away."

"What do you have in mind, boss?" Frank asked.

"Tom, is there a way out through the back of the cabin?"

"A window," Tom said. "But it was a tight squeeze, even for me. The girls could get through it, but none of the men in there could."

"Then the only way they're gonna get out is through the front door," Ned said. "And that means they aren't going to get out. All right, it'll be light soon. Let's go down there and wait for them."

It finally quit raining, but Ned was already thoroughly soaked. Because of the clouds the sun didn't show, but the sky turned from black to a leaden gray. Finally night withdrew from all the notches and draws, leaving behind tendrils of mist to cling to the treetops and hang onto the tops of the hills.

The front door of the cabin opened and one of the men came outside. It was the breed, and he stood alongside the door to relieve himself. Frank raised his gun.

"I can shoot him," Frank said quietly.

"No, not yet," Ned answered. "If we shoot him, they'll kill the two girls for sure."

The breed went back inside the cabin.

"What are you gonna do now?" Tom asked.

"I'm going to give them a chance to surrender," Ned said. He cupped his hands around his mouth and called to the cabin. "Priest! Shelby Priest!"

Even from this far away, they heard an exclamation of surprise from the cabin. It was obvious that Priest and his men thought they were completely safe.

"Priest!" Ned called again.

"Whatta you want?" Priest called back.

"I want you and your men to surrender."

"I don't know who you are, mister," Priest shouted.

"But we got two girls in here with us. Iffen you don't back off, we're gonna kill one of 'em."

"My name is Ned Remington. I'm a United States marshal," Ned said. "I'm here to arrest you and your men."

Inside the cabin, Priest blanched when he heard the name. "Remington," he said. "That's Ned Remington."

"Who is he? I never heard of him," O'Neary said.

"Sure you have," Priest explained. "He's the one been after Passmore all this time. They say he's like a bulldog, once he gets his teeth on your neck, he don't never give up."

"What are we gonna do?" O'Neary asked.

Priest looked over at the two girls. "Them two girls is our only chance," he said. He moved over to the window and cupped his hands around his mouth.

"Remington!" he called.

"I hear you, Priest."

"Remington, you better get out of here!" Priest shouted. "You better get out of here or we'll kill one of the girls!"

"You don't have anywhere to go, Priest," Ned said. "Give it up. Give it up now."

"We gotta show 'em we're serious," Priest said. "Get that one." He pointed to Clara.

O'Neary grabbed Clara, who started to scream in protest. O'Neary tightened his arm around her neck to the point that she couldn't utter a sound.

"Drag her to the door so's they can see you," Priest said. O'Neary did as he was directed. "When I give you the word, cut her throat."

The door opened, and O'Neary stood in it, holding one of the girls in front of him. Ned recognized her as Clara, the older of the two girls.

"I warned you what I was going to do, didn't I, Marshal?" Priest called to him. "This girl's blood is on your hands, not mine."

"Priest, you don't have a chance, why don't you . . ." Ned stopped in mid-sentence when he saw what happened next. O'Neary pulled his knife across Clara's throat and a bright, red stream of blood poured from the slash. O'Neary dropped her, then stepped back inside. Clara fell to the ground and flopped around a couple of times, then lay still while a spreading pool of blood flowed from the wound in her neck.

"My God!" Milsap shouted.

Ned felt himself gag, and he turned away and grabbed a tree for support. He was dizzy and weak in his knees, and felt as if he would vomit. He sucked in air to quell the queasiness in his gut.

"That little girl dyin' is your fault, Marshal!" Priest called. "We done it just to show you we're serious. Now I got another'n in here, an' she's next, iffen you don't back off."

"What'll we do now?" Frank asked. "Do we back off like he said?"

"No," Ned replied. "It's come too far now. We're not backing away."

"Marshal," Priest called. "Marshal, I got me a spyglass in here, an' I done seen somethin' interestin'. You got Lou Wyland with you, don't you?"

"What if I do?" Ned called back.

"Is he the back-stabbin' sonofabitch that turned against his ole' friends by tellin' you where to find us?"

"Maybe," Ned said.

"No!" Wyland shouted. "No, Priest, I didn't tell em . . . ."

"Shut him up," Ned said, and Frank pointed his gun at Wyland.

"I find it awful interestin' that Wyland is ridin' with you," Priest called.

"Deputy Wyland has been a big help to us," Ned said.

"What . . . what are you saying?" Wyland said. "I'm not a deputy!"

"What's going on, Marshal? Where are you headed?" Milsap asked.

"Yes, sir," Ned went on. "He was the one helped set up the ambush with the wagons . . . we nearly got you that time. And he was the one told us about this cabin. He said you'd be here, and here you are."

"Wyland! Wyland, you are a treasonous sonofabitch!" Priest called. "If this was wartime, you could be shot for doin' this."

Wyland took a breath as if to call back to Priest, but Frank cocked his pistol and the metallic click of the turning cylinder got his attention.

"I don't think the marshal wants you to talk to him," Frank said calmly.

"What you got in mind, Ned?" Tom asked.

Ned looked at Wyland, then back toward the cabin.

"I'm trying to make Wyland, here, a valuable piece of property," he said. "I want it so that Ned wants Wyland more than he wants the girl inside."

"No!" Wyland gasped. "No, you can't do that to me."

"Hey, Marshal!" Priest called from the cabin. "Give me Wyland."

"I can't do that, Priest. He's one of my deputies," Ned said.

"Give him to me, or I'll kill the girl."

"I'll make a deal with you," Ned said.

"No deals."

"I'll give you Wyland, you give me the girl."

"My God, no!" Wyland said. "He'll kill me! Don't you understand? He'll kill me."

"I'm sure he will," Ned said. "I'm also sure he'll kill the little girl. What's he got to lose? He killed the other one."

"Please," Wyland said. "Don't do this."

"What about it, Priest? Wyland, for the girl?"

"No," Priest said. "But if you give me Wyland, I won't kill the girl."

Ned looked at the others. "What do you think?" he asked. "Shall I give him Wyland?"

"I say do it," Tom said. "It might buy us a little time."

"Yeah," Frank agreed. "We know damn well he'll kill the girl, we saw them do it with the other one. I don't see that we have any choice."

"I don't agree," Milsap said. "You have no right to leave Wyland to them."

"Maybe so, but like Frank said, I have no choice," Ned said.

"This is clearly in violation of the law," Milsap protested.

"Not my law," Ned said.

Milsap's eyes narrowed. He wiped a sweaty palm on his trousers leg. He opened his mouth, shut it. Remington's face was impassive as stone.

"What do we do now?" Frank asked.

Ned looked at Wyland, who was standing there, shaking in fear. "Give Wyland a pistol," he said.

"A pistol? You're going to leave me with one pistol against three of them?"

"Right now, I suspect the little girl inside would give just about anything for a pistol," Ned said.

Tom pulled an extra pistol from the saddlebag of one of the horses, and handed it to Wyland. Wyland took it with trembling hands, then looked at it as if he had never seen a pistol before.

"Come on, Wyland, I know you know how to use it," Ned said.

"You can't do this," Wyland mumbled. "You can't do this to me."

"Priest?" Ned called out.

"Yeah?"

"We're pulling out," he said. "We're pulling out, and we're leaving Wyland behind."

"Well, now, Marshal, you're finally beginning to show some sense," Priest called.

"Let's go," Ned said, quietly, to the others.

"No . . . no, you can't leave me here like this!"

"Marshal, I don't know," Milsap protested.

"Milsap, do you have a better idea?"

"I . . . I guess not," Milsap admitted.

"Then let's go."

Ned led his men away from the cabin. After they had gone about one hundred yards, Ned stopped them.

"Tom, you remember the window you crawled out of? You think you can get back in that way?"

"Don't know why not," Tom said.

"Good. I want you to circle back around the cabin, come up on their blind side, then get in through that window. Get the drop on them if you can. When you have them covered, fire a signal. We'll come."

"All right," Tom agreed. Tom left then, to make a slow crawl, Indian-style, to come up on the blind spot behind the cabin. Ned, Milsap, and Frank spread out to wait for Tom's signal.

From his position about one hundred yards away, and slightly elevated from the cabin, Ned watched as Priest came toward Wyland.

"Lou," Priest called. "Lou, why did you leave us? You was like a brother to me, didn't you know that? You was a brother to all of us."

"Stay away, Priest," Wyland called. His voice quavered, edged into high pitch.

Priest's voice, by contrast, was smooth as oil.

"Oh, now, Lou, come on. Why are you acting like this? We should be friends, me an' you. You remember when we killed that old woman in Arkansas? Me an' the other boys have a taste for the young ones . . . we didn't want anything to do with her. But you wanted her, Lou. Remember that? You wanted her so we let you have her. Now, this is how you repay us."

"I did it," Wyland said. "But I didn't like it. You know I didn't like it."

"Why, who are you trying to convince, Lou, boy? Me an' you is friends, remember?"

"That sonofabitch," Tom said. "He was taking on about how innocent he was when all along he's as guilty as they are."

"Stay away from me, Priest. Stay away from me, I mean it," Wyland ordered.

Priest kept walking toward Wyland, smiling and holding his hand out toward him. There was no gun in Priest's hand, but Ned and the others could see that Wyland was holding the gun Tom had given him, behind his back.

"Are you afraid because you told the law where to find this cabin?" Priest asked. Priest laughed. "Well, don't be afraid of that. Someone was here the other day, he might've told anyway. I'm not mad at you about that. I just want us to be friends, that's all."

Wyland brought the gun around and pointed it at Priest.

"Don't take another step," Wyland said. The gun wavered in his shaking hand.

"Haw," Priest laughed. "Look at you. It's all you can do to hold the gun up. You think that's got me scared? Why, you probably couldn't hit me, even if you pulled the trigger. You better put that thing away. You're shakin' so much you're about to pee in your pants."

"All this talk about being my friend," Wyland said. "You think I believe that?"

Priest laughed, and pulled on the lobe of his mangled ear.

"Well, now, I guess not," he said. "Lou, boy, I guess the time has come for me to tell you the truth. And the truth is, me an' the others are gonna have a fine time with you. You remember Gitano, the breed, don't you? He knows ways to kill real slow. So, why don't you make it easy on yourself and just come on back with me. I'll tell Gitano not to make it last quite as long."

Wyland held the gun out toward Priest. He looked as if he was trying to pull the trigger, but was unable to. The gun shook badly. Priest laughed, then started toward him.

Suddenly Wyland put the gun to his own temple and pulled the trigger. There was a flash of bright orange light, then a spray of red as the bullet burst through the other side of his head. The sound of the gunshot reached Ned, just as Wyland crumpled to the ground.

"That crazy bastard shot hisself," Frank said.

"My God!" Milsap said. "What did he do that for?"

"I guess he didn't have the guts to face Priest," Ned said.

"You sonofabitch!" Priest yelled, kicking Wyland's

body. ''You sonofabitch! Why did you do that? Why did you do that?''

Screaming, and yelling, Priest kicked and stomped Wyland's body, taking out his blind rage on someone who no longer feared him.

Chapter Eleven

During the time Priest was occupied with Wyland, Tom Beck, moving like an Indian, managed to crawl all the way around the cabin. He was now in position behind the little shack. Signs of the filth in which the men lived were scattered about everywhere. There were skins, feathers, and bones from game animals the men had killed and eaten. There was the sour smell of urine and the overwhelming stench of human excrement, evidence that, like animals, the men relieved themselves anywhere they felt the need. Taking shallow breaths and moving cautiously to avoid the offal, Tom finally reached the position to rise up and look through the back window. O'Neary and Gitano stood near the cabin door. The two outlaws were looking through the door at Priest. Priest, enraged by Wyland cheating him of his revenge, was still cursing and kicking Wyland's body.

"He's downright riled, ain't he?" O'Neary chuckled to his partner. "Look at him kick ol' Wyland around, and Wyland can't even feel it no more."

Gitano, who was standing very close to O'Neary, was holding on to the second of the two Moberly girls. This was Holly, the youngest of the sisters. She didn't look as if she had been hurt yet, but her face was contorted with such pure terror than Beck wondered if the girl would ever recover from the ordeal.

Leaning forward, Tom poked his gun through the window and got the drop on the two men.

"All right, you two bastards hold it right there!" he called.

"What the hell?" O'Neary shouted, spinning around. When they turned, the two men saw the deputy holding a pistol through the window. "Where the hell did you come from?"

Gitano pulled Holly closer to him. He tightened his arm around her neck and held his knife to her throat.

"What you think you can do now?" Gitano spat.

"I think we can take you three men back to Missouri an' stretch your neck a mite," Tom said. Tom fired his pistol as a signal to Ned that he had the drop on the outlaws.

Gitano backed into the corner of the cabin, pulling the girl he still held, along with him. He kept her between him and Tom, so the deputy couldn't get a clear shot.

"You gonna get this girl killed," Gitano said menacingly.

"Please," the girl begged. Her eyes were wide with fear, her lips trembled. "Please, don't kill me."

Tom knew then that he had made a mistake. He did have the drop on them, but he was outside, looking through the window. He realized that if Gitano tried something, there would be nothing he could do to stop him. If he was inside, he would be more effective.

"Hurry up, Ned," he called.

O'Neary chuckled, a low, evil, chuckle.

"What the matter, deputy? You gettin' scared standin' there, holdin' that gun on us all by yourself?"

*   *   *

Priest, hearing the signal shot and Tom's call, started back to the cabin, but Ned and Shaw had been moving in closer and closer on him during his furious outburst against Wyland's body, and before he realized it, they were upon him with guns drawn.

"Go ahead, Priest," Ned invited. "Try and run." He cocked his pistol and levelled it toward Priest's head.

Priest, realizing that he didn't have a chance, put his hands up. He smiled at the three men who were now walking toward him.

"Well now," he said. "So it takes three of you to capture ol' Priest, does it?"

"Call the others out of the cabin," Ned ordered.

"I'll call 'em for you," Priest said. "But that don't mean they'll come out. They pretty much do whatever they want. That's always been the way with us. We're gentlemen of choice."

"Gentlemen? Mister, trash like you and that scurvy in the cabin aren't authorized to even say the word gentlemen," Milsap said angrily. He hurried over to Clara's body, then knelt beside her. The girl's eyes were open and even in death, filled with terror. There was a bloody gash on her throat and blood all down her legs. It was obvious she had been raped before she was killed.

"She's dead?" Ned asked.

Milsap nodded. "My God," he said, closing his eyes and turning his face away. "How could you butchers do something like this?"

Priest looked at the young girl's twisted body and it was obvious that the pathetic sight meant as little to him as if it had been a stick of firewood lying there.

"Dyin' is a part of life," he said. "It's gonna happen to ever'body."

Milsap raised his pistol and pointed it at Priest.

"I'll have none of your trite homilies, sir!" he shouted angrily.

"Yeah, well, it's just too bad you fellas couldn't of come up here in a more friendly way," Priest said. He grabbed hold of himself. "I might'a been convinced to share a little of that with you. She was fine. She was just real fine."

"You sonofabitch!" Shaw said, cocking his pistol.

"Not now, Frank," Ned said. "Tom?" he called out.

"Yeah, Ned."

"You still have them covered?"

"Yes."

"Send them out through the front door."

"We have a problem," Tom said.

"What?"

"The breed is holding a knife to the girl's throat."

"Mr. Remington, please don't let him kill me," Holly called in a high-pitched, terror-filled voice.

"Hold on, Holly," Ned said. "We're just outside."

"They . . . they killed Clara," Holly said.

"I know, honey," Ned answered. "We didn't get here in time to help your sister."

"Back off, Marshal," O'Neary called from in the house. "Back off or we're gonna kill this girl."

"You don't have anywhere to go, O'Neary," Ned said. "You and the breed come on out now."

The door to the cabin opened and O'Neary stuck his head out and looked around.

"That's it, come on out," Ned said.

"You really the law?" O'Neary asked.

"Chief Marshal for Judge Samuel Parkhurst Barnstall's Federal Court," Ned said.

"What you aimin' to do with us?"

"We're going to take you back to Stone County,

Missouri,'' Ned said. "You're going to stand trial there, then you're going to hang.''

"Hangin' ain't to my likin','' O'Neary said. "I gotta think that over a bit.''

O'Neary drew his head back inside, as if to confer with Gitano.

"Don't be all day about it,'' Ned called.

"No . . . no . . . please!'' Holly suddenly called. She screamed, then ran out the front door holding her hand to her neck. Blood squirted through her fingers and gushed down onto the top of her dress. She took several wobbling steps, then collapsed.

"My God!'' Tom choked from behind the cabin. "He cut her throat, Ned! O'Neary held her and the goddamned breed cut her throat!''

"You sonsofbitches!'' Frank shouted, raising his gun.

Russell Milsap began throwing up.

Tom Beck came running around the corner of the cabin, cold-eyed, ready to shoot the outlaws dead in their tracks.

"Tom! Frank! No!'' Ned shouted, stopping them just short of killing the outlaws.

"Let me kill them!'' Tom pleaded. "Scum like this don't deserve to live.''

"No. And they don't deserve a quick death by a bullet either,'' Ned said. "Can't you see that's what they want.''

Priest started laughing.

"Hey, now,'' he said, whooping with laughter and slapping his knees. "If this here ain't the funniest thing I've ever seen, I don't know what is. The marshal havin' to stop his own men from committin' murder.''

Ned had his own pistol out. He walked over to stand in front of Priest.

"Quit laughing," he said coldly, quietly.

Priest was laughing so hard now that tears had come to his eyes. "What do you mean? You gotta admit it's awful damn funny, you havin' to protect us from your own men," he said.

"No," Ned said. "That's not funny." He turned as if to walk away from Priest, then suddenly spun back, and using the butt of his pistol as a club, brought his arm across in a vicious swipe at Priest's face. The gun caught Priest in the mouth, and teeth and blood flew as the outlaw went down under the blow. He fell only to his knees but Ned put him the rest of the way down by clubbing him a second time. Priest fell on his face in the dirt, his arms spread out to either side. "This is funny," Ned said.

As if taking their cue from their leader, Frank Shaw and Tom Beck clubbed O'Neary and Gitano on their heads, knocking both of them out. The three outlaws lay in the dirt alongside the two girls. The only difference was the two girls were dead, the three outlaws were merely unconscious.

"Why," Milsap asked, looking at the two girls. "Why did they kill the girls?"

"Because they are animals," Ned said.

"Ned, you don't really intend to take them back for trial, do you?" Tom asked. "Let me kill them."

"A bullet's too fast," Ned said. "I want them to die slow, and I want them to think about it for a while.

"Then I'll use a knife, " Tom said. "I can use the same knife they used. I could skin 'em while they're still alive, Ned. They'd die real slow an' real painful."

"Tom, don't keep on me about it," Ned said quietly. "You don't know how much I want to let you do what you say. But the law holds me in its

grasp, you know that. If I did this, I'd be goin'
against everything I've always believed in."

"I wish they'd made a fight of it," Frank said.

"I have to confess," Ned went on, "it's eating at
me to have to take these prisoners back to Judge
Barnstall in Galena, put them up at government expense, pay to have a trial, then pay a hangman before
they finally die."

"Marshal Remington?" Milsap said quietly.

"Yeah?"

"Promise me they'll hang," he said. "I want to
see these swine eliminated as badly as any of you.
But you must promise me they'll hang . . . you
won't shoot them."

Ned sighed. "I promise you, Counselor," he said.
"They'll hang."

"Thank you."

When the prisoners finally came around, Shaw
pushed shovels into their hands.

"What's this for?" Priest asked.

"Graves."

"Our'n?" Priest wanted to know.

"For the girls," Shaw said. "And Wyland. We
won't be leaving them lyin' out here."

Sweating, and complaining the entire time, the
outlaws dug the three graves. The two for the girls
were close together, Wyland's was several feet away.

"What are we going to put the bodies in, Ned?"
Tom asked, looking at the two young girls who were
now lying side by side in death. Milsap had cleaned
off the blood as well as he could and now one could
almost think the girls were sleeping.

"Take the blankets and ponchos off their horses,"
Ned suggested.

"Wait, you can't do that. If it gets cold, or it
rains, we'll need those," Priest complained.

"I hope it comes up a blizzard," Ned replied.

A few minutes later the three bodies, now securely wrapped in blankets and ponchos, were lowered gently into the graves. Russell and Frank closed the graves, shoveling dirt atop the bodies until there were three mounds, then Milsap asked for permission to say a few words over them.

"Sure," Ned answered. "Go ahead."

Milsap said a few words, reminding God of the short life the girls had lived on earth, hoping they would find their reward in heaven. The three marshals paid respectful attention to the words, when Priest suddenly grabbed Milsap around the neck, started dragging him over to the edge of a hill.

"Ned!" Frank shouted.

"Don't come any closer!" Priest cautioned. "I'll break his neck if you do!"

"Marshal, never mind me," Milsap gasped. "Even if it means my death, don't let him get away."

"He won't get away," Ned said. "I promise you that. Keep the other two covered," he ordered quietly.

If the other two outlaws held out any hope for their own escape, they were out of luck, because they suddenly found themselves looking down the barrels of two .44 caliber pistols.

"We ain't goin' nowhere, Marshal," O'Neary said quickly, throwing up his hands.

"Oh, I'm sure you're not," Ned answered calmly.

Priest dragged Milsap with him to the edge of the hill. Then Milsap, with a quickness and strength that even surprised himself, pushed Priest away from him. Priest fell over the edge of the hill into the top of a pinetree which broke his fall. Grabbing the limbs of the tree, he shinnied down to the ground. Once he was on the ground he started running, certain now that his getaway would be successful.

"Look at the sonofabitch run," Tom said.

"The man acts like he's going somewhere," Ned said with no show of emotion. Slowly and calmly, he walked back over to his horse.

"Marshal, don't let him escape!" Milsap said excitedly.

"He won't," Ned promised. He looked at the other two prisoners. "Keep an eye on them," he told his deputies.

"What are you gonna do?" Milsap asked.

"I'm going to stop Priest."

"How? He's got too good of a head start."

"I'll find a way," Ned said. He pulled out his Henry repeating rifle, then walked over to the edge of the hill. Priest was still running hard, getting farther and farther away, and growing more and more sure of himself. Ned licked his finger, and held it into the breeze.

"Not much of a breeze," he said.

"Comin' from the north, I'd say," Frank put in.

"You're right. This ought to take care of it," Ned said. He made a slight adjustment to his rear sight.

Tom chuckled. "Say, If you just let him run, you think the sonofabitch would run all the way to Mexico?"

"I expect he'd try," Ned answered.

Ned sat down on a flat rock, crossed his knees, then raised his rifle to his shoulder. On the floor of the draw, now some 200 yards away, Priest was still running

"Are you going to kill the bastard?" Tom asked.

"Not if I can help it," Ned answered. "I'm hoping to just wing the sonofabitch."

"You can't wing 'im from here," Shaw said. "You're liable to miss and you'll wind up killing him."

"Could be," Ned agreed.

Ned took a deep breath, let half of it out, then drew a bead on the running figure. After a long moment, he squeezed the trigger. The rifle roared and rocked him back. A puff of smoke drifted out from the end of the barrel and when it rolled away, Ned could see Priest lying in the dirt.

"Good! You killed the bastard," Tom Beck said.

"No," Ned said. "I hit him in the lower leg, just where I aimed."

Priest lay on the ground for a long moment.

"Priest," Ned called. "You better come on back here."

"I can't," Priest said. "I'm shot."

"Come on back," Ned called again. "Or I'll put a bullet in your other leg."

Slowly, painfully, Priest got up, then started limping back toward Ned and the others. He pulled himself back up the side of the hill, then, a moment later, was in front of them. His right leg was bleeding from a wound below the knee.

"Get on your horse," Ned ordered. "We're going back."

"Why didn't you kill me?" Priest muttered.

"I told you, Priest. You're going to hang," Ned said resolutely.

Priest pulled himself onto his horse.

"Yeah?" he answered, boastfully. "Well, you ain't got me hung yet, so I wouldn't go sendin' out no invitations."

"Let's go," Ned ordered.

Priest winced with pain. "I need some doctorin' done to my leg," he said. "You're the law, you gotta look after it."

"Take a look, Tom," Ned suggested.

With his knife, Tom cut off the bottom of Priest's

trousers. He saw the entry and exit wound of the bullet.

"The bullet ain't in there," Tom said. "But the wound is liable to fester up some before we get him back."

"Enough to kill him, or just enough to lose his leg?" asked Ned.

"Maybe enough to kill him," Tom said.

"You got any idea about what to put on it?" Ned asked.

Tom looked at the wound for a moment longer, then he smiled.

"Yeah," he said. "Yeah, I got an idea." Tom looked through the outlaw leader's saddle bag till he found what he was looking for. He pulled out a small sack of salt.

"This'll prob'ly hurt some, but it'll stop the festerin'," he said. He began pouring salt on Priest's wound, then rubbing it in. Priest grimaced and turned white with the pain, but he hung on while Tom finished his work.

"There," Tom said. "That ought to take care of it."

Ned saw that his deputy was smiling, really smiling, when he climbed onto his horse.

Chapter Twelve

"There," Ned said. He pulled on the rope he had just finished looping around Gitano's neck. The three outlaws were tied together by an ingenious series of ropes and slip knots. "I guess we're ready to go."

"You can't tie us together like this," Priest said. "What if one of the horses was to stumble? Just one stumble an' we'd all have our necks broke."

"Don't stumble," Ned said coldly. Ned mounted his own horse then, and the party started riding away. Behind them, in front of the cabin, there were three fresh mounds. Two, close together, were the young Moberly sisters. Another, off by itself, was the grave of Lou Wyland.

They rode in silence for several moments, then, following the path of the river, rounded a bend so that the house was no longer visible. They started down a long, rock-strewn slope.

"Careful through here," Ned said. "You wouldn't want your horse to trip, now."

"This ain't right, Marshal," Priest complained.

"What ain't right?"

"Loopin' us together like this. Why don't you keep us covered with your pistols? We ain't goin' nowhere."

"I like using the rope," Ned said. "Look at it this

116

way, Priest. Something tells me you were born for the rope.''

''I don't mind gettin' shot,'' Priest protested. ''But I don't want my neck broke.''

''Why don't you quit your bellyachin'?'' Tom called. ''Just what the hell you think we're gonna do with you when we get you back to Missouri?''

''We ain't back there yet,'' Priest said. ''And I figure we ain't gonna make it back.''

''What makes you figure that?'' asked Tom.

''I figure we're gonna get you so pissed off you'll just go ahead an' shoot us,'' Priest said. He chuckled. ''Ain't that what you figure, O'Neary?''

''Yeah,'' O'Neary said.

'' 'Course, bein' the law 'bidin' citizens you are, it's gonna pain you some oncet you up an' shoot us,'' Priest went on, ''but I reckon that's what's gonna happen.''

''We're not going to shoot you,'' Ned said.

''Yeah? You don't sound none too convincing to me,'' Priest replied.

After they were well underway, Milsap fell in alongside Ned Remington.

''I thank you for not letting your deputies shoot these men back there at the cabin,'' he said.

''They stopped themselves,'' Ned said, ''so don't give me credit for it.''

''I can see why someone in a job like this . . . in a position where you encounter these kind of men, might cause you to . . . forget . . . your duty.''

Ned looked over at Milsap. ''Don't you be worrying about that,'' he said. He looked at the three sullen riders, sitting their mounts so carefully in order to keep from tightening the nooses around their necks.

They stopped at high noon, made a cold camp. Lunch was jerky and water but neither Ned nor his men had much appetite. Priest complained though. He said that as prisoners, they were entitled to be fed more that a strip of dried beef and a few sips of water.

"Priest," said Tom, "if I had my way we'd just throw the three of you in a cell somewhere. I wouldn't give you any food or water, but I'd come down every day just to watch you die. When you died, I'd turn a pack of wild dogs loose on you so I wouldn't have much to clean up. So don't be complaining about your food and water. Be glad you're getting anything at all."

It was late that afternoon before Priest started talking, bragging about some of his exploits. Ned knew what Priest was doing . . . knew he was trying to goad him or the deputies into helping them escape the rope . . . even if that escape meant dying by a bullet.

"Say, O'Neary, you recollect that wagon we stopped three, maybe four months ago? The one with the woman that just had a baby?"

"Yeah," O'Neary said. "Yeah, I do recollect that." He laughed. "That's the time when we tied the woman to her husband so's he could be right there when we showed her what a real man could do for her."

"You know, I almost hated to kill them," Priest said. "If it hadn't of been so much trouble to take 'em along, I would'a let them live."

"You killed them?" Milsap asked. "Are you confessing to the killing of an entire family?"

"Not an entire family," O'Neary said. "We left one of 'em alive."

"Yeah. We didn't kill the baby," Priest said.

"What happened to the baby?" Milsap asked.

O'Neary laughed. "Well, they wasn't none of us equipped to take care of it, if you know what I mean."

"What?"

Priest giggled. "The baby needed a tit to suck on," he said. "We didn't happen to have none handy."

"What did you do with the baby?"

"What the hell do you think we did with him? We just left him there, lyin' in the wagon alongside his mama and daddy. Don't know whatever happened to him."

"I have never encountered more degenerate filth than you three men," Milsap said, horrified.

"I like the nuns," Gitano said.

Priest laughed. "Yeah, they was good too. It's been near 'bout a year ago, since we had them nuns. A whole year an' you still thinkin' about that, Gitano?"

"Was good," Gitano said.

"Nuns?" Milsap said, nearly choking in his anger. "You raped some nuns?"

"They was three of 'em," Priest said. "Only one of 'em was so old and drawed-up, ugly, that we shot her right away. The other two we took to our cabin an' tied 'em on the bed, side by side."

"We kept 'em for three days," O'Neary went on. "They was prayin' an' callin' to Jesus."

"You should'a seen Gitano," Priest said. "He went from one to another, back an' forth, back an' forth for the whole time we had 'em."

"You know, the thing is," O'Neary said. "I always had it in my mind that them two nuns was a'likin' what we was doin' for 'em. You know, nuns, they don't have no men aroun'. You know that they gotta get to wantin' it ever' now an' again."

"You 'member what that one said just before you cut 'er throat, Gitano?" O'Neary asked. "She said she forgave us."

"Yeah," Priest said. "I guess that plumb riled me more'n anything. That pious bitch tellin' us she forgave us."

"You bastards!" Shaw shouted. He grabbed Gitano's foot and jerked it up, tossing Gitano off his horse. The other two outlaws, seeing Gitano go down, had to throw themselves off their horses to keep their necks from being broken. With the three men lying in the dirt, Shaw leaped off his horse and began pummeling O'Neary. The ropes tightened around the necks of the other two outlaws.

"Pull him off! Pull him off!" Priest shouted.

Ned stopped, then swung down from his horse as slowly and deliberately as if he were dismounting in front of a general store. He handed his reins to Milsap, then walked over to where Shaw was working over O'Neary.

"That's enough," he said. "Let's ride."

Shaw snorted, kicked O'Neary one last time, square in the crotch. O'Neary doubled over. Gitano and Priest gagged as their nooses tightened.

"We may as well camp here," Ned said, when they stopped again, near sundown. He looked around. "That's a nice cottonwood grove, we can find some firewood in there. Got the river here for water."

"We rode some ground," said Beck.

"What do you make it, Tom? About two more days ride will bring us into Galena?"

"About two days," Beck answered.

"Marshal Remington, aren't you going to . . ." Milsap started, but Ned held up his hand to silence the young barrister.

"Frank, you want to get a fire laid?" Ned asked.

Shaw nodded, headed for the grove of trees.

"Russell, you take care of the horses," Ned said.

Milsap took the horses, led them away to a place where he could hobble them for the night.

Ned got some bacon, beans, and coffee from the saddlebags, and started carving off thick pieces of the meat.

"You got no right to let one of your deputies act like that," Priest said, still rankling over the events at the noon stop. "He could'a beat O'Neary to death."

"If I'd been in charge, I would've helped him beat O'Neary and Gitano both to death," Tom said. "Then I wouldn've started on you."

"You're the law," Priest said. "You have to treat us square, accordin' to the law."

"When did you become such an authority on the law?" Ned asked.

"It's just that I know they's rules for how you treat prisoners," Priest said. "And one of them rules is you don't beat up on 'em."

"Yeah," Ned said. "Well, that's why I stopped him."

"You near 'bout didn't stop him soon enough. I'm glad you'uns is stoppin' here for the night, though. It's mighty uncomfortable ridin' all day long with a rope around your neck. Besides which, I was gettin hungry."

"How can you talk about eating, after the stories you've been telling us?" Milsap asked. After securing the horses, Milsap had found a log to sit on and now he was holding his head as if he was going to be sick.

"What's one got to do with the other?" Priest asked. "Killin' is killin', an' eatin' is eatin'."

"You all right, Russell?" Ned asked gently.

"I . . . didn't know such men existed," Milsap said. He looked at Priest and the others, including O'Neary, who was just now beginning to come around from the beating Frank had given him. All afternoon the man had ridden in a stupor, as if addled. "I can only say this. To prosecute a man who faces the prospect of death by hanging is an awesome responsibility. But with you men, it will be a joy. I will dance a jig as the ropes tighten around your necks."

Frank came back into the camp with an armload of firewood. He looked over toward O'Neary, who drew back in fear of another attack.

"Keep that crazy man away from us," Priest said.

Frank laid the wood for their fire, then lit it. A moment later flames danced and leaped against the circle of rocks he had constructed. Ned lay four slices of bacon in one pan, opened a couple of cans of beans and put them in another. He hung a coffee-pot from a hooked limb.

"You only cut four pieces of meat for the seven of us?" Priest asked.

"This is our meal, not yours," Ned said.

"What are you talkin' about? You gotta feed us."

"Feed 'em, Tom," Ned said.

Beck unwrapped some jerky and carved off three strips. He threw a piece to each of the prisoners."

"What the hell is this?" Priest demanded. "You expect us to eat this while you're eatin' bacon an' beans?"

"You don't have to eat it," Ned said. "You can go without."

"Here," Ned said a few moments later, offering a chunk of dried chili pepper to young Milsap. "The beans always go better with a pepper."

"Thanks," Milsap said, accepting the offer.

Frank got up, poured himself a cup of coffee, then brought the pot around and poured another cup for the men. He sat back down alongside Ned.

"Sorry about goin' a little out of control a while back," he said. "But listenin' to them tell about the rapin' and killin', an' thinkin' about what they done to those two little girls back there, I just couldn't take it anymore."

"Boss, I'm about the same way," Beck agreed. "I just don't think I can stomach another day with these sonsabitches. They're worse'n rattlesnakes. A rattlesnake's only doin' what nature intended it to do. I can't believe nature intended men like this to live."

"How do you feel about this, Milsap?" Ned asked.

"You've gone after outlaws before," Milsap said. "Are they all like this?"

Ned took a swallow of his coffee before he answered.

"No," he said. "I've brought in some men, even faced a few down in gunfights, that had some spark of decency in them. There've been others that you was hard-pressed to find any good to them. But in all my years on the law trail, I've never run in to any like these men."

"You remember Billy Chase, don't you, Marshal?" Tom said. "Robbed a bank up near Independence."

"Sure do. Holed up in a cave over on the Current River when we caught him. Said we'd never take him alive, and we didn't."

"I remember that case," Milsap said. "He killed a teller and a guard when he robbed the bank."

"They tried to kill him," Ned said. "It doesn't justify his killing them, because he shouldn't have been holding up a bank in the first place. But at least it was a reason."

"You remember what we found out about the money he stole? Where it went?"

"Yeah. He tried to give it to the woman that raised him," Ned said.

"Even someone like that, someone who shot down two men, both husbands and fathers, even someone like that had a little good in him. You think there's anything like that in these men?"

"I couldn't say," Ned answered.

"Sure you can say," Tom went on. "Ned, they're lower'n any skunk you ever run across and you know it."

Ned sighed and looked at his deputy.

"All right, Tom, out with it. What are you trying to say?"

"Let's kill them," Tom said. "I was in the Judge's office with you when he gave you the warrants, remember? I know what kind of leeway you got with these men. He said he wanted them dead or alive. They'd be a lot easier to pack in dead . . . and I'd feel a lot purer for bein' the one that did it."

"Tom's got a point, Ned," Frank put in quickly. "Look at them over there. They been talkin' and gigglin' 'bout all the killin' an' rapin' they done all day. I'm sick of it."

"They're trying to goad us into shooting them," Ned said.

"All right, let's say they succeeded," Frank said quickly. "I think we ought to put a bullet in their brains right now."

"Only trouble with that is, they ain't got no brains," Tom replied.

Ned tossed out the grounds that were in the bottom of his cup, then stood up and walked over to where the three prisoners were tied. He pulled out his pistol and pointed it at them.

"Marshal, no!" Milsap called. "You promised me they would hang."

"So, you're going to shoot us, are you?" Priest said. He closed his eyes. "Well do it and to hell with you!"

Ned cocked his pistol and the cylinder rolled, locked into place. He lined the sights up on Priest's forehead. Priest snickered.

"Like the little nun said, Marshal. I forgive you."

Suddenly a hot fury passed over Ned. A fury that couldn't be satisfied by a quick, easy bullet. He let the hammer down, then, with a loud curse, slammed the gun back into its holster.

"You ain't gonna shoot them?" Tom asked, disappointed.

"No," Ned said. "I said they were going to hang, and that's what they're gonna do."

Chapter Thirteen

Ned Remington took the last watch so it would be his lot to see the sun come up the next morning. He had sat for over two hours with his back to a rock and the coals of a small campfire before him.

On a grassy knoll to his right, Milsap and the two deputies breathed softly as they lay wrapped up in their bedrolls. Down from the knoll on a sandy flat, slept the three outlaws. Their blankets and ponchos had been used to bury the dead back at the cabin so the three men were lying on the bare ground, snoring loudly.

Maybe it was the snoring.

Ordinarily, snoring didn't particularly bother him. But it was the fact that these three men, having raped and butchered two young girls could sleep the sleep of the innocent, snoring away as if their consciences were clear.

Ned listened to them snore, and he tossed small twigs into the fire, watched the eastern sky grow lighter until, finally, a blood-red steak of cloud streamed across the horizon. Ned filled the coffee pot with water from the river, measured in a few ground beans, then hooked the pot on a forked branch and waited for it to boil.

A doe came down to the river to drink. It stood by the water's edge for a long time, holding its head up, looking and sniffing all around. It seemed to sense some danger, but thirst was driving it to water.

A haunch of deer meat would make a good supper, Ned thought. He reached for his Henry, slipped it out quietly, and raised it to his shoulder. He sighted over the barrel, drew a bead on the animal's heart, then lowered the rifle.

"Go ahead," he said quietly. "Get your water, I won't bother you."

As if the doe had heard him, she trotted on down to the river's edge and began drinking. A moment later a fawn ran quickly out of the thicket of trees and joined its mother, drinking deeply.

Ned watched until the deer were gone, then he stood up and stretched. He walked over and kicked Tom Beck, lightly, on the sole of his boot.

"Wake up," he said. He moved over to Frank Shaw, then to Russell Milsap, kicking each in turn, lightly, on the soles of their boots. "Wake up," he said to each of them.

Tom sat up and rubbed his eyes, then he looked over at the three outlaws.

"They still alive?" he asked.

"What do you think?"

"I was hopin' they'd get snake-bit durin' the night. Or maybe get struck by lightnin'," Tom said.

"Ned, I gotta tell you right now," Frank said. "If they start in braggin' again today about all the girls they've raped and all the people they've killed, they ain't gonna live 'till night. And if I gotta kill them then turn myself over to you an' go back an' face the judge for murder, why it'll be worth it."

"Only there'll be two of us goin' back," Tom said.

"Can't you fellas see what they're tryin' to do to us?" Ned asked. "They're tryin' to get us so riled up that we'll shoot them. They want a quick, clean, death.''

"I told you, Ned," Tom said. He took out his knife and raked it back and forth on the sole of his boot. "I can arrange to kill them so slow that they'll be cussin' their mothers for ever givin' them birth. It don't have to be quick."

"We should not descend to their level," Milsap said.

"You heard them yesterday, Milsap," Frank said. "Was you enjoyin' what they was sayin'?"

"No, of course not," Milsap replied. "But that doesn't matter. We are the law, don't you see that? Ned Remington is a United States marshal, I'm a Federal prosecutor, you two are sworn officers of the court. Why, we're practically a judicial circuit in our own right. We must respect the law."

"You're right," Ned said. He rubbed his chin and smiled. "You're right about us being practically a judicial body of our own." He got up and walked over to the coffee pot and poured himself a cup. He looked down at the three outlaws who were still asleep.

"There's four of us, three of them. That's seven people and I've seen towns incorporated with fewer people."

"What are you gettin' at, Ned?" Frank asked.

"Yes, Marshal, what *are* you getting at?" Milsap wanted to know.

"I'm going to walk down to the river for a few minutes," he said. "I want to think about something."

"What about our prisoners? Should I wake 'em up?"

"Not yet," Ned said.

Carrying his cup of coffee, Ned walked down to stand by the side of the river. He watched the water as it flowed by in a quiet whisper. A fish jumped. That was its mistake, because a moment later an eagle swooped down out of the sky, stuck its claws into the water, then climbed back up with the fish securely in its grasp.

Ned thought about the scenes of nature he had witnessed this morning. The deer coming for water, the fish in the river, the eagle and its breakfast. There was a natural order to things, if things were left undisturbed. Occasionally someone would come along and the natural order would be disrupted. Young girls would be killed before their time, nuns, who wanted only to pray and be of service to their religion, their beliefs, would be raped and murdered, a young man and woman would have their baby taken from them, then be humiliated and killed.

Those things were not part of the natural order, and when the natural order was disrupted, it should be put right again as quickly as possible. Priest, O'Neary, and Gitano, would have to be removed from this life so that their little corner of existence was set right once again.

Of course, he thought, that was exactly what was going to happen to the three outlaws once they returned to Missouri. In the meantime, they were going to be costing the taxpayers money. And their constant bragging about the horrible crimes they had committed, would cause Ned and his deputies, and young Milsap, a great deal of pain. No sensitive man could listen to their blood boasts without being affected. In fact, one didn't even have to be overly sensitive. One needed only to be sane to know the horror of what these men had done. Not to recognize it would be a mark of insanity.

Insanity.

Ned looked over toward the three outlaws, still

sleeping. Were they insane? Never mind that, it didn't matter whether they were loco or not. The real question was would the court find them not guilty by reason of insanity? If so, would they escape their just punishment?

"No!" Ned said aloud. He started back toward the encampment. "No, by God, no! They won't escape the gallows on a damned technicality."

"Marshal, you all right?" Tom called to him.

"Oyez, oyez, oyez," Ned called aloud. "This territorial court is now in session!"

"What are you talking about?" Milsap asked.

Ned looked at the outlaws. They were just now beginning to stir to wakefulness.

"Gentlemen," Ned said. "I have decided that I cannot take a chance on these men getting away. Therefore, I intend to declare this camp a court."

"A court?" Milsap asked, puzzled by the remark.

"That's right, Mr. Prosecutor," Ned said. "What we have here is a full-fledged, genuine, one-hundred percent federal court, fully empowered to try, sentence, and execute these three men. We'll hold trial right here under God's own sky."

Priest jolted fully awake then, and he prodded the other two men. "Better listen," he said.

"Are you serious?" Frank asked.

Ned looked at the three prisoners. "I'm dead serious," he said. "We are going to try these three men right here. And after we find them guilty, we are going to hang them from that cottonwood tree right over there."

Priest, O'Neary and Gitano blanched. In the morning light, their faces looked gray as mud-clay at a spring. "You can't do this," Priest said. "You got no right to do somethin' like this. I thought you were

the great lawman, never one to go against your
ideals. What you're talkin' about is a lynchin'.''

"Oh, no. It's going to be legal," Ned said. "As
our esteemed prosecutor pointed out to us, we have
all the makings of a court right here. Milsap is a
prosecutor, Beck, you and Shaw are government
witnesses.''

"And what does that make you?" Shaw asked.

Ned looked at the three outlaws and smiled broadly.

"I'm going to be the judge and the jury," Remington said.

"Marshal, I must protest this," Milsap put in
quickly. "No matter what you say, none of this is
legal.''

"If Judge Barnstall was here an' he wanted this
done . . . would it be legal then?" Ned wanted to
know.

"Why, yes, I suppose so," Milsap said. "I suppose the judge could hold court here. The court could
be convened wherever he happened to be, as long as
it was within his jurisdiction. Which, in his case,
would be anywhere in the territories of these United
States.''

"Then consider this court legal," Ned said. "Judge
Barnstall gave me broad powers in this case. He gave
me the authority to bring these men back to him dead
or alive, and he gave me full discretion to decide the
most expedient way of accomplishing my task. I also
happen to know that he wants these men hanged. I'm
acting on his behalf when I say we are going to have
a trial.''

"What about a defense counsel?" Milsap wanted
to know. "The accused are entitled to a defense
counsel.''

Ned looked at the three outlaws. "All right," he
said. "Just so you don't think I don't do things

proper in my court, I'm giving you your choice. You can have Tom Beck here as your defense attorney, or you can have Frank Shaw. Now Tom is part Indian, you might think that would be in your favor, particularly as Gitano is a breed. On the other hand, I think the Indian part of Tom is shamed by Gitano and angered by the fact that most of your crimes have been committed on Indian land. So, you might want to take that into consideration.''

While Ned was touting the attributes of Tom as a defense council, Tom was glaring at the outlaws.

''On the other hand, you might want Frank Shaw. Frank is a mite older than any of you. I expect he's seen just about everything and probably has more compassion than any of the rest of us. On the other hand, old men sometimes get a little cantankerous and you never know what they might do.''

''You're crazy,'' Priest said. He pointed to Tom and Frank. ''You're tellin' us we got to take our choice between these two men? They both hate our guts.''

Ned smiled, broadly. ''Well, now, Mr. Priest. Do you honestly think you can find anyone, anywhere, who won't hate your guts?''

''Nevertheless, no man ain't a lawyer, lessin' he believes you're innocent. An' Shaw knows damn well we ain't innocent.''

''Mr. Milsap, you're the prosecuting attorney in this case. You are also the only one of us with a degree in law. Tell me, is Priest telling the truth? Does a man's lawyer have to believe his client is innocent?''

''Certainly not,'' Milsap replied. ''It is only necessary that a lawyer provide the best defense possible under the circumstances.''

Ned looked at Shaw. "Do you swear to defend these men as best you can?" he asked.

"Yeah," Shaw replied. "I'll do the best I can by them."

"All right, there you go. Priest, you fellas got yourself a lawyer," Ned said. "Frank, you go over there an' talk it over with your clients. The rest of us will stay over here outta earshot. It wouldn't be fair for us to know what your plans were."

"All right," Frank agreed.

"By the way," Ned added. "I wouldn't be recommending that you throw yourself on the mercy of the court, 'cause I can tell you right now, this court sure as hell won't have much mercy."

Frank walked over to the three men and squatted down beside them. Within a few moments they were engaged in an animated conversation.

"I can't believe you are actually going to go through with this," Milsap said.

"Believe me, Counselor, I am going through with it," Ned replied.

"It's a farce."

"No," Ned said. "It's justice."

"But there is no legal precedence for such a thing," Milsap insisted.

"Oh, but there is a precedence," Ned said. "Once before, when a man was leading several others through the wilderness he found it necessary to conduct a trial, then execute the guilty."

"Where?" Milsap asked. "Where can you find such a precedence?"

"You'll find it in the Bible in the book of Exodus," Ned said. Chapter 32, verse 27, when a leader ordered his men to strap on their swords and kill their brothers, friends, and neighbors, for disobeying God's law."

"You're talking about Moses," Milsap said. "He was representing God."

"I reckon that's true," Ned said. "But out here, in this wilderness I am Moses. And believe me, Counselor, to The Nations, the man I represent, Judge Barnstall, is God."

Milsap rubbed his hand through his hair in exasperation, then looked over at Frank Shaw. Frank was still squatting down beside the outlaws, still discussing their case with them.

"What kind of a defense do you expect him to come up with?" Milsap asked. "He not only isn't trained for the law, he hates those men."

"Frank Shaw may not have read for the law," Ned said. "But he's got more common sense than any man I've ever known. Sure, he may hate those men, but he has a sense of fair play and he'll give them the very best defense he is capable of giving. You yourself said that is all that's required."

"Yes," Milsap agreed. "That's all that's required."

"Now, since you're going to have to prosecute, I suggest you quit worrying about Shaw and start preparing your own case."

'What's there to get prepare?" Milsap asked. "This is an open and shut case."

"I wouldn't underestimate the defense counsel if I were you," Ned said. "If I know Frank Shaw, he's going to make you work to get a conviction."

"You're the judge," Milsap said. "Are you telling me there's a chance there won't be a conviction?"

"Milsap, if Frank Shaw gives it his honest best, and his best is good enough that you can't make your case, then you're damned right there won't be a conviction."

"I can't believe you'd do that," Milsap said. "I can't believe you would let these killers off scot-free."

Ned smiled menacingly. "Don't misunderstand me, Counselor. I didn't for a moment say I would let them off scot-free. I said there wouldn't be a conviction. But I'm going to hang these bastards, one way or the other. So if you can't get a conviction . . . it's going to be murder."

Chapter Fourteen

The eagle that had enjoyed a breakfast of fish earlier in the morning, returned to search the river waters. Below the majestic bird's flight path a strange scene was taking place on the bank of the river.

Seven men, isolated from their fellow creatures by many miles, dotted the bank in a precise manner. One man was sitting authoritatively upon a log of driftwood. Another stood to one side of the log, holding in his hand a book, while still another squatted a few feet away. There were three men who were shackled together at their ankles, and a seventh, whose white hair showed him to be the oldest of them all, conferred earnestly with the men in shackles.

"Gentlemen, without the services of a bailiff, I now call this court into session," Ned said.

The three prisoners, at the ungentle prodding of Frank Shaw, stood.

"Shelby Priest, Alex O'Neary, and Hector Gitano, you are hereby charged with two counts of murder and one count of rape. How do you plead?"

"Your honor," Shaw said. "Before we say guilty or not guilty, I'd like to remind the court that I ain't got no proper schoolin' in the whereas's, wherefores, and all that."

"I'll take that in mind," Ned said.

"Yes, sir, I thank you for that. And if you don't

mind, your honor, seein' as Mr. Milsap, who is proper educated, has a copy of one of them lawbooks with him, I'd like him to read to me what the book says about murder.''

"The court so instructs," Ned said.

Russell Milsap cleared his throat, then turned to the proper page in his red leather-bound book. He cleared his throat.

"The law of homocide," he read. "Section 3, Criminal Homicide. Criminal homicide is homicide without lawful justification or excuse. Paragraph A. Murder. Murder is homicide committed with malice aforethought.''

"Mr. Prosecutor, so that there be no misunderstanding of the term, would you please define the phrase 'malice aforethought?' '' Ned said.

"Yes, your honor," Milsap said. This is sub paragraph 1. The use of the words malice aforethought must not be permitted to obscure the result. As a matter of law a killing may be with malice aforethought although it is conceived and executed as rapidly as thought can be translated into action.''

"Thank you, Mr. Prosecutor," Ned said. "Are you now satisfied as to the definition?''

"Yes, sir," Shaw answered.

"How do your clients plead?''

"We don't plead nothin' '' Priest spoke up. "This here ain't no court an' you got no right to try us.''

"Gentlemen," Ned said coldly. "I have the right, because I have the might. Mr. Milsap here, who was educated in the fine institution of Washington University in St. Louis, will tell you that might makes right is common law . . . law as old as Moses. Now, either you enter a plea of not guilty, or you confess your guilt and throw your miserable carcasses upon the mercy of this court. And, as I told you earlier, *this court has no mercy!*''

"We ain't guilty!" O'Neary said quickly.

"Counselor, is that the plea you are entering on behalf of these men?" Ned asked Frank.

"Your honor, if you don't mind, I'd like young Mr. Milsap to read me one more thing out of his book."

"All right," Ned said. "What do you want read?"

"I want you to read to me about how a fella's not guilty if he's insane," Shaw said.

"Insane? Are you callin' us insane?" Priest shouted angrily. "Look here, where do you get the gall to call us crazy? You got no right."

Ned looked over at Milsap. It was obvious that the young lawyer had not expected this particular approach and was both surprised that Shaw thought of it, and dismayed that he might have to contest it.

"Mr. Milsap, will you read the information for us?"

Milsap looked in the index of his book, then thumbed through the pages. "This is chapter 8, section 2, paragraph C," he said. "To establish a defense on the ground of insanity, it must be clearly proved that, at the time of the commission of the act, the party accused was laboring under such a defect of reason, from disease of the mind, as not to know the nature and quality of the act he was doing; or if he did know it, that he did not know that what he was doing was wrong."

"Thank you," Frank said. "Your honor, my clients ain't guilty because they was insane."

"The plea would be not guilty, and not guilty by reason of insanity," Milsap said.

"Thank you, Mr. Prosecutor," Ned said. "You may now present your case."

"Your honor," Milsap began. "This court intends to prove that the defendants, Shelby Priest, Alex O'Neary, and Hector Gitano, did, with malice afore-thought, kill Clara and Holly Moberly. This court will also prove that the defendants, Shelby Priest, Alex O'Neary, and Hector Gitano, did commit rape upon the person of Clara Moberly, Clara Moberly being a minor at the time. Prosecution calls its first witness, Mr. Tom Beck."

Tom, who had been squatting the whole while, stood up and walked over to stand in front of Ned Remington.

"Raise your right hand, Tom," Ned said.

Beck's hand went up.

"Do you swear to tell the truth, the whole truth, and nothing but the truth, so help you God?"

"I do."

"Would you tell the court your name and current occupation, please?" Milsap asked.

"Thomas W. Beck. I'm deputy to Ned Reming-ton, Chief United States Marshal for Judge Barnstall's court."

"Mr. Beck, I ask you to look at the three defen-dants and identify them for the court."

"The tall thin one with the mangled ear, that's Shelby Priest. The one with red hair is Alex O'Neary, and the halfbreed Creek and Mexican is Hector Gitano."

"Let the court note that deputy Beck has correctly identified the defendants," Milsap said.

Milsap turned his back to Tom, then walked toward the three defendants. He fixed them with a steely stare. This was his first case, and it was being tried on a sandy bank alongside a river near a stand of cottonwood trees in the middle of Indian territory. Yet he brought all the dignity, honor, and skill he possessed to bear on the proceedings. Had he been arguing this case in the halls of the Supreme Court, he would not be giving more of himself than he was now.

"Mr. Beck, would you please tell us when you saw these men for the first time?"

"I seen 'em first at their cabin near Chetopa," Tom said.

"This was before the murders we are trying?"

"Yes," Tom said. "I was pokin' around in the cabin. It was filthy, an' from the looks of things, they'd had women out there before. Prob'ly tortured, an' maybe murdered them."

"I object, your honor," Frank said. "That don't have nothin' to do with what we're tryin' for today."

"Sustained," Ned said.

Milsap looked up in surprise. He hadn't expected Shaw to put up any objections. Maybe he isn't trained in law, he thought, but his common sense had apparently told him that the material Tom was giving wasn't germane to the case under consideration. And Ned Remington sustained his objection. It could be that this really was going to be a trial.

"Very well," Milsap went on. "We'll move forward to the next time you saw them. Where was that?"

"Well, that would be on the trail between Coffeyville and Joplin. As you recall, we'd joined our wagon up with the Moberlys. Me an' Ned was sleepin' while you an' Shaw was on guard. I was woke up by the girls' screamin' an' when I looked around I seen these three men draggin' the girls off with them."

"By girls, who do you mean?" Milsap asked.

"Well, I mean Clara and Holly Moberly."

"The same two girls who were later killed?"

"The same."

"And did you go after the girls?"

"Yes. We sent the Moberlys on to Joplin while the rest of us set out after them three. We caught up with them at the cabin, the same cabin I'd seen 'em at before."

"Now, Mr. Beck, tell the court what happened when the men were cornered in the cabin."

"Ned here, he identified hisself as a U.S. marshal. Priest told him if we didn't leave, he was gonna kill one of the girls."

"And what happened next?"

"They just cut her throat," Tom said coldly. He looked over at Priest. "They just cut her throat and left her to flop around in the dirt like a chicken with its head cut off."

"Which girl was this, Mr. Beck?"

"It was the oldest one, Clara."

"What happened next?"

"Marshal Remington, he tried to trade Wyland for Holly. That's the girl that was left."

"That would be Lou Wyland, a one-time associate of the Priest gang who was helping us?"

"Yes," Tom said. "Anyway, Ned tried to trade Wyland for Holly, but Priest wouldn't do it. So Ned, he sent Wyland down anyway. Wyland went down to the cabin, then he shot hisself. While they was all lookin' at Wyland, I crawled around back of the cabin and looked in through the window. I got the drop on them an' ordered them to surrender."

"And did they surrender?"

"Yes, they surrendered," Tom said. He looked over at the three men and glared at them with such hatred that it was almost physical. "But not before they cut the second girl's throat like they done the first. She was screamin' and beggin' all the while, but that didn't make no never mind. They just cut her throat slick as a whistle.''

"Thank you, Mr. Beck. Your witness," he said to Frank.

"Mr. Beck, was we lookin' at them when they cut the first girl's throat?''

"Right at them," Tom answered.

"And was we lookin' at them when they cut the second girl's throat?''

"We was lookin' right at them that time, too.''

"Thank you," Frank said. "That's all.''

Milsap's next witness was Frank Shaw. To his surprise, Frank stepped out of his role as defender of the three men and provided testimony every bit as damning as that provided by Tom Beck. And, like Tom Beck, he glared with hate and anger at the outlaws during his time on the witness stand. When Milsap completed his direct examination of the witness, he turned to Ned.

"Your honor, I would now, normally, turn my witness over to the defense counsel. But, as this *is* the defense counsel, I'm not certain as to the procedure.''

"Your honor, while I was a witness for the prosecution, I was the best witness I could be," Frank said. "Now, I'll be the defense counsel again, an' I'll do the best I can do in that job.''

"Very well, Counselor, you may continue," Ned said.

Looking straight out from the witness area, as if he were in Judge Barnstall's court in Galena, Frank went on.

"I want it understood that, as a defense counsel, I would ask myself these questions. Was I lookin' right at these three men when they killed the first little girl? The answer to that question is yes I was.

The second question is, was I looking right at these three men when they killed the second little girl? The answer to that question is also yes, I was lookin' right at them. That's the only two questions I have of myself.''

Milsap next called Ned Remington to the stand.

During this direct examination, Ned completely separated himself as witness, from himself as judge and jury. On the stand he was respectful and dutiful, making no effort to direct the questioning in view of his self-appointed position in this court.

When Milsap was finished with Ned, Frank Shaw asked him the same two questions he had asked of Beck and himself. The answer from Ned, was the same as it had been from Beck and himself.

Milsap was his own witness. In his own words he told, step-by-step what happened from the time he joined the marshals until the men were cornered in their cabin. He told of witnessing the murders of the two little girls.

In his cross examination, Frank asked the same two questions, and got the same two answers.

''Your honor,'' Milsap said then. ''The prosecution has no more witnesses to call.''

''Very well, Mr. Milsap. Defense, you may now call your witnesses to the stand.''

''Thank you, your honor. I call Shelby Priest to the stand.''

''I'm chained to these here other men,'' Priest complained. ''Are you gonna unlock me so's I can come up there?''

''No need to,'' Frank answered. ''They can come with you.''

Growling, Priest hobbled up to the place that had been designated as the witness stand. His walk was hampered not only by the chains, but by the wound from the bullet hole Ned had put in his leg the day before.

"Priest, how many men have you killed?"

"Just men? Or ever'body?"

"Everybody."

"Injuns and Mexicans counted?"

"Every human bein'."

"Well, hell, I don't count Injuns or Mexicans human bein's," Priest said.

"What about Gitano?"

"He's half Mex, half Injun," Priest said, as if explaining something to him.

"Do you count him as human?"

"No."

"But he rides with you. He's your friend."

"He rides with me, but he ain't no more my friend than my horse."

"I see. You ain't answered my question. How many people have you killed?"

"Your honor, I must protest this," Milsap suddenly said. "I've gone along with this because I thought Shaw was genuinely doing his best to defend these men. Now he's asking how many people his client has killed. That is very obviously going to prejudice the court against his client."

"You got a reason for asking this, Frank?" Ned wanted to know. "I mean a reason that benefits your client?"

"Yes, sir."

"Answer his question," Ned said to Priest.

"I can't answer it," Priest said.

"Why not?"

" 'Cause I don't know how many I've kilt. I mean, that's like askin' me how many times I've took a leak in my life. Who the hell keeps count of things like that?"

"He's your witness, Mr. Milsap," Frank said.

Milsap, surprised that Shaw had turned the witness over so quickly, was slightly taken aback. Nevertheless he recovered quickly, and walked over to stand in front of Priest.

"Mr. Priest, did you kill Clara Moberly?

"Was that one of them little girls?"

"Yes. It was the first girl that was killed."

"No," Priest said, smiling triumphantly. "O'Neary, he kilt the first girl an' Gitano, he kilt the second one."

"You sonofabitch! You told us to do it!" O'Neary swore.

"Is that right, Mr. Priest?" Milsap asked.

"Mr. Priest," Priest said, laughing. "Don't know as I ever been called mister before."

"Is he right? Did you order the killing of the two girls?"

"Well, yeah, I reckon I did. But I didn't do it myself."

"It doesn't matter whether you did it yourself or not," Milsap said. "It doesn't even matter if you ordered it done. You were a party to it, a co-conspirator, and therefore you are as guilty as the person who actually wielded the knife."

"Haw!" O'Neary said. "How does that set with you?"

Priest glared at O'Neary, then at Milsap.

"I have no further questions of this witness, your honor."

"What do you call it when I want to ask him somethin' else?" Frank wanted to know.

"Redirect," Milsap answered.

"I got me a redirect," Frank said.

"Go ahead."

"Priest, when you know'd that we was lookin'

right at you, me, Marshal Remington, Lawyer Milsap, an' Deputy Beck, when you seen us lookin' right at you, why did you kill them girls? Didn't you know we would see you and testify against you in court?"

"That wasn't somethin' I was thinkin' about," Priest said.

"What was you thinkin about?"

"I don't reckon we was thinkin' about anything," Priest said.

"O'Neary? What was you thinkin' about? Why did you do it when you know'd we was right there watchin' you?"

"I don't know," O'Neary said. "It didn't mean nothin'. I mean, hell, like Priest said, we done kilt so many now, what's another'n more or less?"

"Gitano? What do you say about it?"

"Kill girl is easy," Gitano said. "It like kill bug."

"No more questions," Frank said.

"Are you ready for summation?"

"Yes," Frank said. Frank pulled out a plug of tobacco and cut off a piece. He stuck it in his mouth then rolled it to one side before he spoke.

"Your honor, you heard me ask ever' witness if they was lookin' right at the prisoners when the girls was kilt, and ever witness said that they was. Then you heard me ask the prisoners why they kilt the girls when we was lookin' right at them, an' they all said that they did it, 'cause it didn't mean nothin' to 'em. Priest said he couldn't count the number of people he had kilt, 'cause it weren't no differn't from takin' a piss. O'Neary said killin' didn't mean nothin' and Gitano said he could kill a human as easy as he could kill a bug. Now, Mr. Milsap, would you read what the book says about bein' insane again?"

Milsap read: "To establish a defense on the ground of insanity, it must be clearly proved that, at the time of the committing of the act, the party accused was laboring under such a defect of reason, from disease of the mind, as not to know the nature and quality of the act he was doing; or, if he did know it, that he did not know that what he was doing was wrong.''

"Thank you," Frank said. He looked at Ned. "Your honor, if we're gonna be honest an' true, we're gonna say that men who think killin' is no different from takin' a piss, or killin' a bug, is suffering from that defect of reason the book was talkin' about. They didn't know that what they was doin' was wrong, and that means they was insane. And if they was insane, then they ain't guilty."

"Mr. Milsap," Ned said gruffly. "I'm goin' to give you five minutes to prepare your summation. And I warn you, Mr. Prosecutor, the defense has made a powerful case for these men. You better be good, sir. You better be damned good."

Chapter Fifteen

During the five minute recess, Russell Milsap went down to the river to dip his cup into the water. As he drank his water, he looked back up the slope at the "court" assembled there. He looked at Frank Shaw, the bullet-scarred, weathered old man who sometimes loaded baggage on stages, sometimes rode as shotgun guard, sometimes made fried-apple pies for little girls, sometimes acted as a deputy . . . and, today, had taught him a lesson in law more valuable than anything he had learned in the hallowed halls of Washington University in St. Louis.

Russell was just beginning his law career. If he lived to be seventy-five, if he argued great and weighty cases in the twentieth century, he would never forget the morning that he, a twenty-three-year-old assistant prosecutor argued his case on the sand and pebble beach of a wild river in the Indian territories. He would always remember the day criminal justice was carried out in a lawless land by men who care about the law and justice.

And now he was up against it. He had to refute the surprisingly strong defense put up by Frank Shaw. "Frank," he said under his breath, "you should have been a professor."

"And from whom did you learn your most valuable

lesson of law, Mr. Milsap.'' Russell imagined some
future conversation might go.

''From Frank Shaw.''

*''That's Dr. Shaw of Harvard? Or Professor Shaw
from Penn?''*

''That's Frank Shaw from Galena, Missouri,''
Milsap would answer.

"Is prosecution ready for summation?" Ned asked.

"I'm ready, your honor," Russell replied. He
slipped his cup back into his saddlebag, then walked
back up the sandy slope to address the court.

"Your honor, gentlemen of the court, that these
men are guilty, there can be no doubt. We are in a
unique position, perhaps never before enjoyed by a
court, of having been eye-witnesses to the very crimes
for which we are charged to try these men.

"Each of us, with our own eyes, watched the
horrible murders of the poor Moberly girls. We have
our own knowledge of this act forever burned into
our minds by sight . . . and, through testimony we
have shared these visions. The sharing was important, because now we are all certain that we saw what
we saw.

"And, if our own eyewitness accounts weren't
enough, we have heard the prisoners condemned by
their own words. They have admitted killing Clara
and Holly Moberly.

"Now, though they do not stand accused in this
court of other criminal acts, we have heard from their
own mouths the most outlandish tales of evil and
perfidy one can possibly imagine. They have boasted
of murders and rapes and obscenities that boggle the
senses.

"In their defense, counsel has suggested that these
men might be innocent, and innocent by reason of
insanity. I think it is important to point out here, that,

even in defense, no attempt has been made to deny the commission of these crimes. They are guilty of all that we have seen and not seen, heard and not heard, and as such, are an abomination to the laws of nature and man.

"So, with that in mind, it now seems proper and fitting to disallow the plea of insanity in order to find these men guilty as charged. But how can we find them sane? For what sane man could commit crimes with such lack of passion?

"The answer is . . . no man could, if we gauge sanity by the standards of moral men. But these men aren't moral, and the only test of sanity we must hold up to the light is whether they were men of reason when they committed the crimes. Reason, gentlemen, for that is the operative word when deciding whether or not a defendant is legally insane. Were these men of reason? Or were they totally irrational in those perpetrated deeds, murder if you will, under judgment by this court?

"I call your attention to a remark made by Shelby Priest when we first happened upon them at their cabin near Chetopa.

" 'If you do not leave', he said, 'I will kill one of the girls.' Your honor, I want you to gauge the full impact of that statement. Priest threatened to kill one of the girls if we didn't leave. His *reason* for that threat, was to force us to leave. He was therefore aware that the threat to kill the girl was one that would disturb us. He could not reason such a thing, unless he had the tool of reason in the grasp of his mind. He could not threaten, if he were not aware that killing was an evil thing.

"Therefore, your honor, I submit that Shelby Priest, Alex O'Neary, and Hector Gitano were fully in possession of reason at the time we surprised them in camp. I furthermore submit that they were completely aware of right from wrong, and knew that killing the girls was a heinous act.

"If you accept this logic, then you must declare the defendants sane at the time of the killing. And, your honor, if they were sane at the time of the killing, they stand condemned by our own eyewitness of their action, by our collective accounts, and by the words issued from their very own mouths.

"If justice is truly to be served in this court of ours, if truth will out here on this lonely sand bank in the midst of some of the most beautiful country God has ever created, then there can be only one verdict rendered toward each defendant. That verdict, your honor, is guilty, guilty, guilty.

"The prosecution rests."

"There will be a brief recess while I deliberate," Ned said.

Tom Beck and Frank Shaw walked over to Russell Milsap. Both were smiling, and both had their hands extended.

"Whooee," Tom said. "I tell you, Milsap, that was some of the best speech-a-fyin' I ever listened to, an' I've gone to a heap of Fourth of July picnics."

"Young fella, you're gonna be a hell of a lawyer," Frank said. "Hell, that's wrong. You're a hell of a lawyer right now, an' I for one am gonna tell the judge what a good man he has in you."

Milsap beamed under the praise of the two men. He was especially pleased to hear the words from Frank.

"I must tell you, Mr. Shaw," he said, "you would have been quite a lawyer yourself. You caught me off-guard. I had no idea you would be able to mount any kind of defense for these men."

Frank rubbed his bewhiskered chin and looked over at the three sullen outlaws. "I tell you, son, I just thought about the thing that I was most worried might happen to get them off if we took them back to Galena, then I used it. I'm glad you was able to knock it down."

"We don't know yet that I did knock it down," Milsap said. "The judge hasn't given his verdict."

"I ain't worried," Frank said.

"This court will come to order," Ned called.

All eyes turned toward him.

"Shelby Priest, Alex O'Neary, and Hector Gitano, stand before the bench."

Frank stood the men up, then positioned them before Ned.

"I find all three of you men guilty as charged. And I sentence you to be hanged by the neck until dead. Sentence is to be carried out immediately. Deputies Shaw and Beck, get the prisoners mounted and moved into position under that large cottonwood. Throw ropes over that branch and place nooses around their necks."

"No!" Priest shouted. "No!" You ain't got no right to do this."

"That issue has been settled," Ned said.

Protesting every inch of the way, the three outlaws were set on horseback and moved into position under the tree. Frank and Tom threw ropes over the limb, then tied and looped nooses around the necks of the condemned trio. All was in readiness.

"Have you men any last words?" Ned asked, looking up at them. He stood on the ground with his feet set wide apart.

"Yeah," Priest said. "Yeah, I got somethin' to say." He looked at Remington and his eyes narrowed to conspiratorial slits. "Remington, I got somethin'

you want bad an' I'll give it to you iffen you let us
go.''

"There's nothing on earth you have that I want
bad enough to let you go," Ned said.

"You want this," Priest said.

Ned nodded at Tom. "Get ready," he said.

"No, wait! I know where Passmore is!" Priest
screamed.

Ned held out his hand to stop Tom.

"You know where he is?" Ned asked in a strained
voice.

Priest smiled. "I know where all his hideouts is
. . . where he stays most of the time. I can lead you
right to him. I'll do it if you let us go."

Remington's face remained impassive. The marshal said nothing.

"Hell then," blurted Priest, "go ahead an' hang
these other two if you got to, it don't make me no
never-mind. But iffen you let me go, I'll take you
right to the man that kilt your wife an' raped your
daughter.''

"How do I know that you even know Passmore?"
Ned asked.

"I can prove it," Priest said.

"How?"

"Your wife," Priest said. "She had a birthmark,
looked like a strawberry, right below her belly-button?"

"How . . . did . . . you . . . know?" Ned asked
through teeth, clinched in anger.

Priest smiled. "I was there," he said. "I didn't do
nothin' mind you. But I was there. Now, that proves
I know Passmore, don't it? An' iffen you'll set me
free, I'll take you to him. You got my word on
that.''

"I have your word," Ned said in a voice just
barely under control.

"That's a fac'," Priest said.

Ned looked over at Frank.

"Haw!" Priest guffawed. "I know'd I could talk you out of it."

"Hang this sonofabitch," Ned said quietly.

Frank startled the horses of the three men and they leaped forward. The ropes pulled them out of the saddles, choking Priest's laughter off into a death rattle.

It was deathly quiet, save for a creaking sound as the men turned slowly at the end of the ropes. It had been nearly five minutes since the horses bolted, almost four minutes since the last twitch from one of the bodies.

"Cut them down," Ned ordered.

Frank and Tom cut the outlaws down and laid them out under the tree. Ned looked over at Milsap and saw a pinched, uncertain expression on his face.

"What's the matter, boy?" Ned asked. "You did your job well. This wasn't murder, this was an execution."

"I . . . I can only say that I'm uncertain about my future in the court," Milsap said.

"After watching you perform today, I'd say your future is very bright," Ned said.

"Not after word of this gets around," Milsap replied.

"There's a simple way to handle that. Don't let it get around. There are some things that are best left unmentioned. We chased them, caught them, and they tried to escape. We killed them. That's all there is to it."

"But there are no bullet holes in their bodies. Their necks are stretched like beheaded chickens and they didn't try to escape," Milsap said.

Remington pulled his pistol, then shot each outlaw once, in the heart.

"Did you not see them on horseback trying to get away," Remington asked Milsap as he blew the smoke away from his pistol barrel. "If they hadn't been tied up to that cottonwood tree, they'd have made it, too."

Milsap sighed in resignation, as Beck and Shaw joined Remington in gallows laughter. Beck and Shaw picked the outlaws up and tied them, belly-down, on the horses Beck had recovered.

"If someone, someday, asks me about how these men died, by whose law their lives were ended, what could I ever say in reply?" the young prosecutor wanted to know.

"Tell 'em Remington's Law," Beck answered.

"This court is hereby adjourned," Remington said solemnly.

CHANCE

The Maverick with the Winning Hand

A blazing new series of Western excitement featuring a high-rolling rogue with a thirst for action!

by Clay Tanner

CHANCE   75160-7/$2.50US/$3.50Can
Introducing Chance—a cool-headed, hot-blooded winner.

CHANCE #2   75161-5/$2.50US/$3.50Can
Riverboat Rampage

CHANCE #3   75162-3/$2.50US/$3.50Can
Dead Man's Hand

CHANCE #4   75163-1/$2.50US/$3.50Can
Gambler's Revenge

CHANCE #5   75164-X/$2.50US/$3.50Can
Delta Raiders

CHANCE #6   75165-8/$2.50US/$3.50Can
Mississippi Rogue

CHANCE #7   75392-8/$2.50US/$3.50Can
Dakota Showdown